LOOKING FOR THE SPARK

And Other Stories by Scottish Writers

1994

INTRODUCTION BY
CATHERINE LOCKERBIE

HarperCollins*Publishers*

HarperCollins*Publishers*
77–85 Fulham Palace Road,
Hammersmith, London w6 8jb

Published by HarperCollins*Publishers* 1994
1 3 5 7 9 8 6 4 2

The Publisher acknowledges the financial assistance
of the Scottish Arts Council
in the publication of this volume.

A catalogue record for this book
is available from the British Library

ISBN 0 00 224349 0

Set in Linotron Baskerville
by Rowland Phototypesetting Ltd
Bury St Edmunds, Suffolk

**Printed and bound in Great Britain by
Hartnolls Limited, Bodmin, Cornwall**

LOOKING FOR THE SPARK

And Other Stories by Scottish Writers

Critical Acclaim for *Scottish Short Stories:*

A Roomful of Birds: Scottish Short Stories 1990:

'This year's volume continues to attest to the vitality of the short story in Scotland'
The Scotsman

'A stunning collection of short stories from Scotland's finest contemporary writers'
Book News

The Devil and Dr Tuberose: Scottish Short Stories 1991:

'Demonstrates the continuing power of the short story' *Daily Mail*

'The *Scottish Short Stories* series generally throws up some strong work and the 1991 version is no exception' *The Scotsman*

The Laughing Playmate: Scottish Short Stories 1992:

'Each one of them has found . . . that secret little lock in the mind's door, the story a key to the opening of new and resonant spaces'
The Scotsman

Three Kinds of Kissing: Scottish Short Stories 1993:

'Admirably demonstrating the art of the perfectly crafted short story' *Options*

'An exhilarating display of skill and story-telling by craftsmen' *Edinburgh Evening News*

CONTENTS

INTRODUCTION

That's what we were doing: looking for the spark. That little fine flash which somehow, mysteriously, snaps light into a story, snaps *life* into it. There's many an accomplished enough piece of writing which still lies inert on the page. For this eagerly anticipated annual volume, we wanted more: not inertia but energy, not empty technical accomplishment but the imagination-firing tinderbox of the true writer.

We found our image of the spark, and a bright example of it, in the title story by Angus Dunn. A young man, labouring at logging, puzzles as to just what makes one of his fellow-lumberjacks so special: there is nothing obviously extraordinary, nothing unusual about him, yet he has a rightness, a grace perhaps, which is not that of other men. Of what does that specialness consist? Where does it reside? How to isolate, name, satisfyingly grasp it?

These are the questions, the crucial questions, that we three judges, Tom Adair, Alison Walsh and myself, had to hold keen and poised in the attention as we sifted through more than two hundred submitted stories. The young logger knows that spark plugs make an engine start; but his friend dismantles a diesel engine, which has no such plugs, which has no one instantly visible cause for combustion. The friend shrugs. 'You start it moving and it keeps going,' he says. 'It goes because it goes.'

So with these stories. The motor must start and carry the writing forward at precisely the right momentum. They must feel ease-ful, necessary, not strained or showing-off (which is anyway forbidden to all Scots from the Calvinist cradle onwards . . .). They must offer complete yet resonant worlds, in which for the space of reading, our imaginations may be entrapped, altered and enriched. Naturally, some of the writers who know how to do this are the practised professionals, and we have some of Scotland's finest here: Candia McWilliam, Andrew Greig, Duncan McLean. Importantly, though, some are new or as yet little known: finding the spark, the essential combustion, is at least as much to do with an inner knowledge, an innate knack, as a learned set of techniques or tricks.

As always, stories were submitted anonymously, a vital way of ensuring too-human judges respond purely to the word on the page and not to perceived reputations. The judging is a pleasurably arduous task, each of us having made a personal selection which is then defended with eloquence only sometimes degenerating into physical violence. (I jest, of course: our discussions are the very model of reasoned and mature democracy . . .) An exciting moment is the unveiling of the authors' names after our final list has been agreed on. We then learn how many of Scotland's most lauded writers we have cavalierly cast by the wayside; we learn if our confident guesses as to the identity of certain distinctive stylists have been correct; and we learn if our list contains an appropriate cross-section of those many people drawn to this most potent and difficult of literary forms.

Thus, we discovered that our choices were statistically dominated by women; that most of these writers have been published before, a good few in previous editions of this volume (an interesting continuity against the odds, as the judges change every two years); that there is a good mix of full-time writers and those who are busy doing 'proper' jobs; that we picked up both members of at least one writerly household – not the partnership of Brian McCabe and Dilys Rose as last year, but that of Andrew Cowan and Lynne Bryan, who live in Glasgow with their daughter Rose (their very different and excellent stories both feature highly sensitized descriptions of pregnancy . . .). In the gap between judging and final publication, we may learn more interesting and good news about those we have selected. Alison Armstrong, for instance, whose 'An Apt Conceit' is a masterly, pungent and ambitious study of an artist of another age, took the £5,000 *Cosmopolitan* short story prize. Alan Warner, whose 'A Dog's Life' is a desperately poignant tale of growing old and vengeful in the heat of Spain, was given a book contract with Cape. We glow quietly with pride and a pleasant sense of vindication.

Award-winners or not, all these writers were chosen because their work spoke and sparked. There's a giddy and gladdening eclecticism in the range of topics and tone. From Angus Dunn's forestry plantation, its rough specificity prickly and resinous, to Gillian Nelson's cold Polish townscape, all icy memory and idealism, to Sylvia Pearson's torrid, heat-and-sex-bound South African garden, these Scottish or Scottish-based authors place no limits on the internal territory of their imagination. If geographical boundaries are leapt with a healthy athleticism, so too are those of class and age. We move from working-class launderette to upper-class below-stairs; from the brilliantly sinister child's-eye view of Iain Bain's 'Entertaining Dorothy', to those same heightened edges of childhood recalled from the vantage point of reflective old age in Candia McWilliam's rich and suggestive 'A Jeely Piece'. Some are funny: Duncan McLean's 'Navigator' is a fine sweet piece of cheek from one of Scotland's most vigorous younger writers. Some are sad: Andrew Cowan's 'Terminus' is a controlled and poignant account of a very public death by heart attack. Some are funny *and* sad: Alison Smith's excellently observed 'The Unthinkable Happens to People Every Day' matches a minor TV personality's thrashing despair against the cool and resurrecting comments of a small, polite girl in a Highland roadside café. Some are uplifting: Jean Rafferty's 'Walk On' is a good old-fashioned solidly constructed story with a lovely humanity at the heart of it.

So does this twenty-second annual collection provide a comprehensive survey of the Scottish soul and the skills of its authors? It can't, of course do any such thing; although the complete set of all the volumes to date might begin to approximate to that lofty ideal. What we offer here is something just as valuable: a string of lights, a line of latent fires, illuminations for the mind and emotions. May they spark for you, the reader, too.

CATHERINE LOCKERBIE

LOOKING FOR THE SPARK

LOOKING FOR THE SPARK

Angus Dunn

Where the road is straight, he lifts his tin from the dashboard. He is steering with his forearms resting on the wheel, his face not far from the windscreen. Gusts of wind batter at the van, but we barely drift from a straight line. Below his chin, his fingers pry open the tin, select a cigarette paper and a pinch of tobacco.

From my seat I can see his eyes concentrating solely on the road ahead, while his fingers carefully hold the makings so that any excess tobacco falls into the tin held between his palms. The skin of his palms is smooth, slightly glossy from the constant friction of the safety gloves. When I check my own hands, they are rough, prickled with a thousand tiny abrasions from the spruce needles and bark. I rub my cheek with one hand. The hand feels bristly, as if it needs a shave.

He was in no way different from other men. When he drove a fence post, he lifted the mell as other men do, pausing at the top of the swing and letting it drop. He did it well, raising himself on his toes at the last moment so that the face of the mell landed flat on the top of the post. The fence post rang as he struck and the earth swallowed another few inches of wood.

When you're fencing, you never go anywhere with empty hands. There's always something to carry up or down the line of the fence. After the first few days you learn. Sometimes you see someone start off, then remember and pick up a roll of wire or a mell. With the more experienced men it shows as just a moment's hesitation.

The squad worked better when he was there, even though he wasn't the foreman. When he had set a post, he never paused: just shouldered the mell, picked up a couple of posts, or whatever was needed, and was off to the next post-hole. The rest of us automatically worked around him, letting him set the pace.

By the time we reach the corner, he has placed the tobacco in the paper and closed the tin. He drops it back on the dashboard and sits up, both hands on the wheel, the paper pinched closed on the tobacco between his index and middle fingers. A shred of tobacco hangs out at one end, rocks to and fro in the draught from the air vent. After the corner, there is a short straight stretch. His wrists rest on the steering wheel, he rolls the cigarette, lifts and licks it, rolls it closed and puts it between his lips, presses in the cigarette lighter. Turns into the bend.

Nor is he unusual in any other way. He shops for himself, buys clothes and food. Perhaps he watches television in the evening. I have seen him in the crowded streets on Saturday afternoon, completely unremarkable among the other shoppers. I barely notice that I've noticed him, until afterwards. Other people, too, move through crowds without being jostled or impeded. It is a skill you learn. Most people learn it, after a while.

Now and then I have seen him in the bar, drinking lager, speaking with the barman, playing pool with his friends, whom I know only by sight. He inhabits a world that is not the same as mine, though they overlap. It's not a large community: I've heard his friends talking, seen them now and then at work. They're a mixed bunch, but none of them are remarkable. None of them is interesting in a way that he is, for all his ordinariness.

*　　*　　*

The lighter clicks and he lifts it to the cigarette, inhales, blows out blue mist. Though I do not smoke, I enjoy the smell of the tobacco smoke mingling with the petrol and oil and the scent of spruce resin and pine sap.

My eyes flicker open and closed. I lapse into a warm doze, unexpectedly satisfied with getting the day's work done, getting the contract finished. Somehow it's more than just labouring when you can see the size of the job, when you can aim yourself at the end of it. I know he's got nothing lined up for next week. My eyes are half closed, but I can see his face. He's not worried. I don't know if I'll find work anywhere else, but I'm not worried either. It must be contagious.

He was cutting a ride through a plantation. I was working to him with the hook, stacking the pulp and the saw logs. The work was hard, the day was hot.

The tree shivered, he pulled the saw out, stepped to one side and it fell. Before the branches had stilled, he was trimming the trunk: brown dead twigs near the base, then thicker green branches towards the top. He sliced the top off and I stepped in with the hook, stumbling on the hag, and turned the tree. He worked down again, trimming the branches which had been underneath. Then he hooked his tape measure on the end, walked along, marking the tree in three-metre sections, then turned and walked back, cutting the tree into pulp logs, while his tape rewound itself. He bent down and unhooked the tape and moved onto the next tree. I dashed in and hauled the logs into a more-or-less neat pile at the side of the ride.

I was doing the unskilled job. Hauling logs across a horrible bouncing mattress of branches lying on rough ground riddled with dead stumps and drainage ditches. And every log was different. The lie of the hag changed with every tree that came down. Logs snagged on a stump or rolled the wrong way. If the stack wasn't right, it could collapse when the new log went on it.

But he had an easy rhythm to his work, going through the same motions again and again, every tree the same. Cut it down, walk once up and down the fallen tree to sned the branches, once up and down to cut it into lengths, then on to the next tree.

Of course, when I tried it myself, I found it took some skill to make the job so dull and predictable. A breeze was enough to send a tree sideways. A first cut that was a centimetre too deep would jam the sawblade. And if it fell backwards into the other trees, it had to be cut down into useless logs, a few feet at a time.

There was nothing remarkable in the way he felled trees. That was a difficult skill to master.

By the time he finishes his cigarette, we are coming down the hill, and I am busy planning what will happen when I get home. It's Friday night and I'm feeling good that we finished the job just at the week's end. There should be good crack at the National tonight, they've got a band on. And Martin's back from the West. There should be a party at his place.

'There's a party up the Heights tonight.'

'Aye?' He acknowledges the statement.

We're coming up to the main road now. He watches the road as he stubs his cigarette out. His face is attentive, he checks both ways. There's nothing to say. He does not speak.

One morning, he didn't arrive to pick me up. I had no phone, so I walked out to his house. He had the engine out of his van and was taking it to pieces.

'Wasn't sounding right,' he said. 'Be a couple of hours.'

I stayed to help, but there wasn't much for me to do. He didn't work fast, he took time to select the right tool for each job, laying the engine parts in a semi-circle around him.

I remember when we dismantled an engine at school, I

had an uneasy feeling that something was missing. All the parts were there, shiny metal bits that slid against each other or spun round each other, but there didn't seem to be anything to make it go. I tried asking the teacher, but he didn't understand that I was looking for some sort of final cause: he lectured me on the expansion of gases. Then I noticed the spark plugs, lying on a bench, and the pieces came together. That was the important bit, the spark that made it go.

As he delved deeper into the van engine, something of the same feeling came back to me. This was a diesel engine. It didn't have a spark plug. I understood well enough that the explosion of fuel and air was caused by sudden compression, but that wasn't a final cause.

When all the bits were spread out, naked and shining, I asked him.

'Where's the bit that makes it go?'

He looked surprised for a moment and I thought he was going to tell me about explosive compression. But he didn't.

'You start it moving and it keeps going,' he said. That didn't help. He must have seen it in my face. He shrugged. 'It goes because it goes.'

That was it. I could grasp that. The core secret of the diesel engine.

'Right.'

He gathered some pieces of engine and began to put them together again, without hurry, but wasting no time.

I wonder what he does at home. Whether it is different from other people that I know. Whether it is unusual, or even interesting.

I imagine it is quite ordinary. There is no local gossip about him and his relatives don't live here. Though they might do. If they were as unremarkable as he is, perhaps no-one would know.

I watch him, try to imagine him with a brother or a

sister. He concentrates on the road, anticipating the traffic well to keep the old van moving smoothly.

We worked for an hour at a time, until his petrol ran out and we stopped to refill. I needed the five minutes' rest. He cleaned his saw and sharpened the chain. It was late in the day and I was tired. I couldn't walk on the hag without stumbling, jamming one leg and then the other amongst the layers of branches. After a short break, he started back along the ride, studying the next tree, while his feet stepped over the snarly branches, avoided the hidden gaps. Landing always on a solid place.

I knew I should move. If he started on a second tree before I cleared the first, I'd have to hook the logs out from under. But I couldn't do it. We'd been working since 5 a.m. to get the cool of the day. I'd stripped down to T-shirt and shorts and my forearms and legs were scraped and bleeding and needle-pricked. My face was burning hot and stinging with perspiration.

He stopped at the tree and started up the chain saw. He leant over to cut, but before he began, he looked to see where I was. He stood up again, his head shaking. It was too far away to be sure, but I think he was grinning. He beckoned me to come on and I stood up. He bent and started the cut.

Before I began moving down the ride I stood for a moment and looked. The spruce needles in the canopy were a dark blue-green from underneath, but where the cut branches lay on the ground, the upper part of the needles was visible, a bright emerald green. There was a blue stripe of sky above the ride, bordered with dark blue-green. Below, there was a brown-walled corridor of tree trunks and a broad bright carpet of emerald green leading to the next tree, where he was a small figure intent on his work.

I stumbled forward on the hag and my mind swallowed the image whole.

*   *   *

6

We're stopping now. He opens the glove compartment, gets out his wallet, counts money onto his knee then hands it to me.

I take the money and check it, because I should, but not really counting. He's reliable.

I stow the money away. The engine is running. I climb out and wave.

He waves back and drives off. There is nothing remarkable about his going.

TERMINUS

Andrew Cowan

Before they saw the man die they were sitting by themselves on a bench at the terminus, sharing a portion of chips and watching the tourists. The man's name was John Cheery, though they weren't to know that until the ambulance came. Then a voice in Billy's head would remark, *Not so cheery now, John,* and afterwards repeat this until he began to feel guilty. Later, he'd include the voice in his anecdote of the death as a kind of confession, unsure if it revealed his maturity or childishness.

Half an hour before he died John Cheery was saying good-bye to his friends in a pub by the harbour. He found them there every summer. They were local men with stony faces and they betrayed no surprise when he appeared at the bar. As he drained his last glass he told them, 'I got one the other night anyway, first for years. Felt rotten afterwards. The wife came and sat on me, in my dream, up there in the digs. She undid me. I always dream about her when I come here.'

'You'd think she'd just leave you be,' the barman had said.

A stream of buses also departed from the terminus that lunchtime, and as their engines ticked over Melanie drummed her fingertips on her belly, which made Billy feel squeamish and nervous. 'There were all these other women there too,' she said, 'and they just stared into space like moon cows, huge great moon cows.' She spoke rapidly, in a voice that was almost a whisper, as if willing her words to escape unnoticed. 'They were all older than me, and the woman on reception was foul, so patronizing, she kept calling me "girlie".' She picked another chip from the nest in his hand. 'Girlie,' she sighed, and slumped a little further on the bench slats.

Their bench was bolted to a shelter of perspex and steel, half a mile from the crush of the people in town. At their backs the land fell away to the shore, which is where they had wanted to be; and where they usually went, though not often in daylight. One evening in May they had met and parted before the last bus had arrived from the depot. The sea had swelled in the darkness, tolling the bells of the buoys, creaking the boats on their moorings. A ferry had shimmered as it rounded the headland, lights had winked from the masts of the yachts. That had been their first time and later they'd descended to the bed of sand in the rocks as if to their own private place. But today the rocks were unstable and the steps had been closed. A web of yellow tape barred their way.

Across the bus-bays in the sunshine stood the Tourist Information Office and the new public toilets. A queue of taxis stretched as far back as the railway station, itself the end of the line, beyond which the town rose steeply, a clutter of churches and trees and flinty grey cottages. Most of the houses now traded as shops and holiday lets. The local folk lived further out, in streets not marked on the sightseeing guides and everywhere else was cars and caravans and coaches. By autumn the car park next to the terminus would be empty, a wide concrete nothing, and Melanie and Billy would be amongst those who remained. Melanie took another chip, and whispered, 'These are disgusting.'

'So don't eat them,' said Billy.

'If I don't eat, I feel sick,' she whispered, and Billy felt the air cool, become darker.

For eleven weeks and three days Melanie had eaten and wept, and when the tears came, it wasn't from worry or fear or simple unhappiness or pain; she wept because that was her condition. She loathed it and quietly cursed as she sobbed, but she could not prevent it. And always beside her, Billy hunched his shoulders and waited. He was sensitive to tears, like a sailor to breezes; he felt their approach like a change in the weather. As Melanie's sobs now subsided she told him, 'I couldn't sleep, I was all hot, I thought I was going to lose it. I had these terrible pains. I kept going to the toilet to see if there was any blood.' Then, taking another chip, she whispered, 'You should've come to the clinic with me.'

'I never know what to do,' he murmured. 'You never say how I can help you.'

On the night his first child arrived John Cheery had gone to bed drunk. In old age he would still remember the price of his beer that evening, and he could recite the date of every penny increase until it reached a round shilling. But he never spoke of his daughter. The labour was early and unexpected and his wife, who was seventeen years old, sent him out through the backs in his pyjamas to find a midwife. But his mind was still clouded and a fog had descended. The air smelled thickly of fermentation and the local brewery stables. In the murk he took a wrong turning, three times hammered the wrong door in identical alleyways. When finally the nurse appeared on her doorstep, holding a candle before her, the baby had already been born. Her birth was the last act of her life. John Cheery buried her in a grocery crate two days later.

In the cool ceramic quiet of the new public toilets Melanie smoothed the front of her dress and faced her reflection. She was wearing dark glasses that hid the smear of black round her eyes and when she removed them she noticed another thing that was new, a flush of red that spread back from her cheeks to her neck. For weeks there had been nothing, no visible sign, but now her appearance was changing, shifting, surprising her from mirrors. In the striped canvas sack that hung from her shoulder she found a tube of lipstick and drew it over her mouth, painted herself older. There was a smell of chip-fat on her fingers. She held her breath.

Billy bundled the wrapper into a ball and tossed it from the shelter. On the pavement outside the Tourist Information Office a bearded man in shorts was making a video film of his wife. She was sitting on a wall and shuffling some leaflets, a bank of shrubbery behind her. The other tourists steered around them but the man still lowered his camera, watched impatiently until they had gone. There was a stack of post-cards in his waistband, flecks of grey in his beard and hair. His wife seemed to be talking to the camera, or at least Billy imagined she must be, because there was nothing in her sur-roundings that he considered worth filming.

On this stretch of coast there was no pier or funfair or penny arcade. The only slot machines sold cigarettes and condoms. But in the centre of the town, at the rear of the civic building, there was a cinema where Melanie worked as an usherette. She had not been trained in courtesy. To the tourists, as she ripped their stubs in two, she presented the same distracted half-smile as she did to those locals who knew her. They would watch her pale sandalled heels as she led the way up the stairs in the dark, seek her eyes when her torch found their seats. She always looked away to the screen; and later, when the film reached its end, she would hurry ahead of them to the exit and down the road to the harbour. Billy sold whelks and cockles and mussels from a trailer parked on the quayside. When he saw her descending he would place a carton of whelks on the coun-ter, lay two wooden forks beside it.

'Lipstick's a bit heavy,' he told her. He raised the brim of his sunhat and narrowed his eyes, but Melanie ignored

him. She fixed her gaze on the man with the camera until
Billy began to feel foolish. Finally he sighed and reshaded
his eyes.

'Help me, Billy, look,' she said then.

Later they would have no memory of John Cheery standing,
taking the air, walking towards them. This was the first
and all they knew of him: an old man slumped on Melanie's
shoulder, neither upright nor horizontal, already dying,
uncontrollably trembling. When Melanie slipped out from
beneath him he didn't topple but continued to shake,
and Billy said, 'Is he having a fit? I don't know what
to do.' Then, to the man, 'Can I help you up? Are you
having a fit?' John Cheery's face was red but not from
the sun.

In the carpeted hush of the Tourist Information Office
Melanie took her place in the queue and waited until the
woman in the blue sweater had transacted a sale. Looking
down, she saw she was standing on the join between a blue
and a red carpet tile, and she stepped backwards for luck,
both her sandals on red. Then on tiptoe she called, 'Excuse
me, but there's a man having a heart attack,' and felt herself
flushing. The other heads were turning to see, but the
woman ignored her, clasped her hands on the desktop. She
smiled to the first in line. 'He's across there,' Melanie
added, again almost whispering, 'in the bus shelter.'

The woman hesitated then, smoothing the front of her
sweater. She glanced abstractedly behind her, to a pale
wooden door marked PRIVATE. 'You go on,' she waved to
Melanie. 'I'll just phone for an ambulance.'

Billy bent to help the man upright, but he was too heavy
to move; not unless he embraced him, which he could
not do. The old man was slobbering now. The tremor in
his chest had carried to his jaw and it was making his
teeth clack, but his gaze was direct and unblinking. Billy

searched his eyes for annoyance, aware that he was young and failing, not wanting his to be the last face the man saw. But there was nothing, no accusation, not even pain or alarm, and Billy heard himself asking, 'What shall I do?' He touched the man's trembling arm, as if this could prevent him from falling. He wondered if he should leave him.

The image fixed in John Cheery's mind as he died was of a woman and two girls. A wind whipped across them as they stepped from their house and the woman hugged her dressing-gown closer around her. She was small and barefoot and wouldn't dress until evening. Her face was worn, without make-up, and in her short pale fingers she held a freshly lit cigarette. She used it to point with, a prod towards the neighbouring house. Her girls hurried from their gate and ran up the next garden. They laughed as they hammered the front door. They were half-sisters and called John Cheery 'Grandad' although they bore no relation. As they shouted through the letterbox the woman stepped into the long damp grass and peered over her fence. She shook her head. She thought she had heard him returning, but the house was still empty.

An old lady was watching from the corner of the bus shelter, her face interested and smiling. When Billy saw her she came closer, as if invited, and placed a hand on his back. She was holding a new brush, the head wrapped in blue plastic. It matched the colour of her frock. 'Perhaps he should be lying down,' she said. 'He doesn't look very comfortable to me.' So Billy crouched at John Cheery's feet and hugged the old man's legs to his side, cradled them as he might a child, awkwardly, self-consciously. The woman propped her broom against the rear of the shelter. She curled a gentle hand behind John Cheery's neck and spoke into his ear. 'Can you talk to me?' she asked. 'Can you say something?' Then to Billy she said, 'I think you should take his arms.'

Billy bore the weight of John Cheery's body but the old man slumped in the middle. His eyes seemed to roll upwards; his face darkened. 'He's very heavy,' Billy said as he lowered him. 'He's had a long life,' the old lady replied.

In the pub by the harbour John Cheery had said to his friends, 'She's never been near the sea, I asked her to come but she wouldn't have it. No one to look after the girls. She couldn't leave them. She was married at nineteen, first time, but he left her. He reckoned the girls weren't his, so he left her. The oldest's eleven, red hair. The other's five and she's dark. Then there's a third on the way.' He winked. 'All different fathers.'

When the cab had arrived to collect him she'd come from her house in her dressing gown and John Cheery had sat in the passenger seat, his door open, whilst she shivered in the damp air. She had given him a bag for the train, some rolls and biscuits, a girlie magazine. Then she had kissed him on the lips and called the girls to come forward. John Cheery pressed fifty-pence pieces into their hands. Before closing the cab door the woman had said, 'Send us a postcard.' And he'd nodded to her fag, her belly, and replied, 'Look after the little 'un.' The driver had coughed as he started his engine.

The old lady felt in John Cheery's mouth for his dentures. She removed his cap, too, and his spectacles, and placed them on the bench at her side. As she wiped her hands on her frock Melanie whispered beside her, 'It's a heart attack. You can tell because of his face. We learned it at work. But I've forgotten everything else.' And they looked to the blue-uniformed woman who was hurrying across from Tourist Information. Her head was down and she was watching her footing, her heels clacking across the bright concrete. With a catch of breathlessness she said, 'I've told my girls where I am,' and knelt carefully beside the old

man. The motif on her sweater said, *We'll show you where,
we'll get you there.* She tugged it over her head, quickly
checked the buttons on her blouse. 'Right,' she said
then, smiling to Melanie. 'Recovery position? Or mouth-
to-mouth?'

Later, Billy would say the man had been dead from the
start, that even if he had recovered he would have been
paralysed on one side, perhaps brain damaged. He would
say they should have allowed John Cheery to die where he
sat, still wearing his cap and glasses, still with his teeth in.
Another day, he would read a book of first aid and satisfy
himself that all their efforts had been futile. He would find
that John Cheery should not have been laid on his front
until his heart had recovered, that his chest should not
have been compressed if his heart was still beating, that
respiration and compression should not have been practised
simultaneously. Later still he would attend classes and
become an expert in practical first aid, but he would never
find another opportunity to use it.

Before she took hold of his wrist and searched for a pulse,
the uniformed woman arranged John Cheery's limbs in the
posture of a climber on a rock face. A rivulet of piss ran
along the gap in the paving slabs beside her and she laughed
as she said, 'There's something here somewhere.' Then she
asked Melanie, 'Can you find it?', and repositioned her
knees on the concrete.

   'I think he should be on his back again,' Melanie
whispered.

In the pub they were interested in John Cheery's neighbour
and asked questions as they accepted his drinks. His face
now coppery with whisky, he told them, 'She moved in the
year after my wife died. She looked after me. I looked after
her. I paid her TV licence first off. The van came round,
so I paid it. Then there was no food for this weekend, or that

weekend, so I helped her. I gave her the money. Because she was crying. Always crying.' Her electricity was about to be cut off, and he gave her £140 for that. Her gas bill was £90. The telephone was more.
'She ever pay you back?' they asked him.
'No, nothing. Never will,' he said.

The woman from Tourist Information laid a neat square of white handkerchief over John Cheery's mouth, left an imprint of lipstick as she blew through it. Billy was surprised to see the old man's stomach inflate. He scratched at his scalp through his sunhat, concentrated his gaze on Melanie as she depressed the man's chest. Her action was gentle and rolling and she made the barest impression. There ought to be more give, Billy thought, but he kept his distance, felt the first onlookers gathering behind him. The old lady bent towards Melanie. 'Keep it going,' she encouraged her, 'you're doing fine, just fine.' Then to the woman, 'I think you should hold his nose. Hold it closed.' Billy watched the swell of Melanie's breasts as she pumped, the smooth contour of the bulge in her dress. Her arms were straight and thin, locked at the elbow, a faint down of fair hair tracing their outline. Sometimes they had pressed down on him like that.

When the holiday season was over they would make their first home in three rooms in the old town. Like the trailer on which Billy worked, the cottage belonged to Melanie's parents, a holiday conversion which had once formed part of a brewery, enclosed and sunless. Shells and sea urchins now hung above the kitchenette in a fishing net. Through a porthole window at the rear it was possible to catch a glimmer of sea. On Saturday mornings for three summers Melanie had gone there to tidy after the visitors, and always began in the bedroom, expectant and hopeful, like the tourists who combed the shoreline every evening at low tide, gathering leavings she would later discard. In the coming autumn it would be Billy who cleaned out the rooms. And whilst he painted the ceilings and doors, pinned pictures to the walls, disinfected the worktops and corners, Melanie would begin to spend nights in her old home; more frequently as the winter deepened. But when her labour began, early and unexpected, she would be lying upstairs in the cottage, practising her breathing. Outside, the fog would smell of the sea, and Billy would run down the hill in his slippers, clutching a handful of coins for the telephone.

There were many noises which might have been the ambulance – horns sounding on the busy seafront road, the reversing beep of buses, the rush of the waves – and each time he heard something Billy felt, as if waking from sleep, a brief moment's alertness before he sank again into numbness. Behind him a voice murmured, 'It only has to come down the road. It would've been quicker to take him on a bus.' And, looking round, he noticed the bearded man with his video camera, not filming now but watching intently, absorbing every detail. Beyond the crowd there was sunshine. The minibuses continued to arrive and depart, depositing tourists from the fishing villages, collecting mothers and children for the housing estates. A few rucksacks and shopping bags had been left unguarded at the bus-bays. As the onlookers slowly multiplied the interior of the bus shelter became darker and quieter, and Billy wondered about the man's name, if there would be any information in his pockets, perhaps about his medical condition, his family, but he watched Melanie and said nothing, felt the distance slowly widening between them.

'Swap?' said the woman from Tourist Information, and Melanie released herself from John Cheery's chest, slumped back on her haunches. She closed her eyes and dropped her shoulders, felt the sweat on her forehead, the dampness in her dress at her sides. Her heart pulsed in her ears, she could hear the sea and the old lady speaking beside her.

'Deep breaths,' she said softly, 'you're almost there.' And wearily Melanie bent to add her own lipstick to the square of white handkerchief. She had not been aware of the gathering strangers, the dimming light and the absence of air. But as she lifted her face now she began to feel her confinement. She tried to inhale. The old man was dead, she was sure. And she hadn't enough breath to share. She glanced around for Billy and found him standing amongst strangers. His sunhat was lopsided. She felt herself tilting also and reached a pale hand towards him.

'I'm here,' he said then, and she was weeping, falling against him as the handkerchief slipped to the concrete.

When the crowd thinned, stepped backwards, there was a smell of salt air and diesel. Billy heard a voice say, 'She's a lovely-looking girl,' and he pressed his nose to the back of Melanie's head, whispered, 'Well done,' so quiet she would not hear him. The bearded man had stepped forward and he was holding John Cheery's wrist, his wife standing outside, tracing a finger on the timetable. The faces of the spectators were dark against the blue sky, and some shook their heads as the uniformed woman fished inside the old man's jacket. She said, 'I suppose he has a name,' and withdrew his wallet, held it up to the light. Then Billy glimpsed the approaching ambulance. It was descending the hill from the town, appearing and disappearing through the stacked green of the trees. 'Here it comes now,' he mumbled. And louder, 'This is the ambulance now. It's coming!' But it was heading in the wrong direction, following a slip road to the rail station. He got to his feet and started to run, heard Melanie's voice shouting behind him to hurry. Outside in the car park a breeze lifted his hat from his head, and for a moment he faltered, but didn't return to retrieve it.

'Does she do anything for you?' the men had asked in the pub, and John Cheery told them, 'I used to play with her.' His teeth clicked and he rubbed at the side of his chin, watching their faces. 'She let me,' he said. 'She let me play with her. But not straight off. There was the girls, she needed the cash. So she used to fetch my shopping – I gave her my wallet and sent her out to the shops. But that cost me, the change was never right, so I stopped it. Then she took my washing instead. Still does. I paid her to do it, pocket money, and I said she could do the ironing, but she burnt my shirts. No good.' He shook his head, spoke quietly. 'This was early on, after the wife died. I was bad then, poorly, but she helped me.' The men nodded, and he said, 'Later she came round nights and she let me touch her. But I couldn't stay hard. He'd go all soft on me. I got close to it once, but I couldn't satisfy her – old man like me. She needed a younger man. I asked her to marry me once, I told her she'd make a good wife if she tried. But she laughed.' He grinned, raised his last glass to his lips. 'She laughed,' he said.

The first paramedic loosened the valve on an oxygen cylinder. 'So what do we know about him?' he asked. And the woman from Tourist Information said, 'His name is John Cheery.'

The large-handled electrodes that sent a pulse through John Cheery's body caused him to jerk from the ground. The sound was a hollow thwack like a slap, and the paramedics repeated this at intervals, the old lady standing over them, patiently waiting. In one hand she held her new broom, in the other John Cheery's cap as if it were a bowl, his teeth and spectacles and wallet inside. Billy and Melanie watched from the sea wall. The black-and-yellow tape whirred in the sea breeze behind them. Melanie's dress flapped at her knees. Billy moved close against her, his chest to her back, and cupped his hands under her belly. 'Shall we go down to the rocks?' he whispered, and she shook her head. She pressed against him, turned her eyes to the ambulance. They saw the sheet being pulled across the dead man's face, heard the tide pulling away from the shore. Billy looked out past the harbour. A ferry glinted in the sunshine. It was rounding the headland, growing out of the distance towards them.

A JEELY PIECE

Candia McWilliam

'Never in my wildest would I have, would you now? Would you indeed? Or would you not?' It was restful to converse with Rhona; the energies that went into the necessary emotions, outrage, offence, dignity, were all hers, but there was an aspect of her talk that was demanding, on this warm day, to Mollie. Something to do with having to keep an eye on the subject, that was apt to change, tuck itself in and rethread with the imperceptible flicker of an invisible mender's needle.

They had known one another all their lives and soon they would be dead, thought Mollie, undisturbed as a teenager in love by the thought of death, whom she thought of as a friend of the family. Dying, though, was more hard to get on with, she could not fancy that. Her ideal would be to be taken after a morning's gentle exercise, gardening perhaps, or a turn round the park, something that would tire her out and reward her curiosity with something to puzzle over so that she would be happily distracted when she was taken. Rhona would die talking, of course, ambling around the subject, approaching it, changing it, holding possibilities up to the light like negatives to check them for light and colour and shade.

Sixty years ago they had spent the night together in a plum orchard. If that was the word? Maybe prunery, or *prunière?* Anyhow, it had been in Rhona's father's plot which he had down to plums, and in which he had built a playhouse for Rhona, with a ladder leading up to a wee platform where you could just fit two camp beds. Downstairs there were three chairs about right for porridge-eating bears, a small dresser and a toy cooker that cooked when primed with paraffin. Matches, though, were to be used only under supervision, so Rhona and her friends tended to take things out to the cooker already cooked, insert them and remove them after a while with expressions of relish such as, 'My word what a crust,' and, 'You must let me have the receipt for that one day soon.'

An indiscriminate archaism was part of the game of the playhouse. Its limitations of scale and equipment demanded further refinements. Especially when the girls began to grow up and to become aware that they were doing so, they worked at setting the playhouse and the games connected with it in times safely past, if they had ever been. The small house in this way became a hallway to expansive ideas and tall dreams.

Rhona was one among brothers, handsome boys with big teeth and eyelashes, who wanted to be lowland farmers like their father. Of course the farm could not be divided, so two of the boys would eventually have to find their own places. They would never go to England, that was a certainty, a place they had been raised to consider the source of all that was not right in their lives, a coward country that, like all cowards, was a bully too. India had been mentioned, and tea planting, if it was not to be Scotland. The number of Scotsmen out there planting the tea was something amazing, it was said, so a man need never be lonely seeking his fortune with the tea.

The timbers of the playhouse were proofed against rot by a protracted soaking in a bitumen tank that was in the woods behind the barn and the byres in a dark grove of ponticum. Over the tarpaulin roof Rhona's father had laid over-and-under pantiles, curved like letter s's lying down, tucked one into the next with a snugness whose pattern satisfied like that of the feathers on an ordinary bird. The windows of the house went out on casement latches that curled at the end like creeper trails.

Rhona's father had an unnecessary streak that made him do things more ornamentally than other men. Her brusque mother was not like this. It could hurt Mollie to see Mrs Gordon overlook on purpose some fillip the farmer had added to the breakfast table, nasturtium flowers in a bowl perhaps, or treacle initials written on the children's oats. Mollie had seen the farmer's wife stir these initials to a blur one day before the children came down, her face disproportionately full of something close to vengeance. She made bread on a Saturday and the farmer liked to make a single plaited loaf that he would decorate with seeds half-way through the baking. When it was done he would lift and tap it as though it were a warm instrument of percussion. He sang out of doors; Rhona said that he was an atheist who kept his eyes open during grace, said by her mother. Mollie had several times spent Christmas with the family, when the farmer said grace himself, looking holy as holy and bringing a kind of conviction to Mollie that did not usually assail her, a desire to be seen to be extremely good, more especially in the eyes of Mr Gordon than the terrible eyes of God.

In the First World War, he had been wounded and one time, not meaning to, at the seaside at Gullane on a tart summer day, Mollie had seen the wound. Or rather she had seen through the upper arm of the father of her friend. It was his right arm, white, and when she saw the hole, which he was drying carefully by patting it with a beach-towel as one pats a sore baby, it reminded her of the separate flesh packets, muscles, that composed the drumstick of a chicken. Mr Gordon had spectacles and a temper, he was tall and thin and grey, but the fear Mollie felt for him did not make her want to avoid him. This feeling grew in her when she saw him drying thin air on the brisk beach at Gullane while they sat on rugs among seaholly and thrift and sharp grass watching the sternly inert sea.

The sandwiches had been meat. Mr Gordon had whittled some driftwood into a dragon shape and shown the children how to extract the bitterness from a cucumber by cutting off the tip and turning it round and round on the cut end till all the white gall had been milked out. He then scooped out the seeds, halved it along its length and handed around sweet chunks of the cold cucumber, improved beyond its vegetable self, transformed into fruit.

When the boys were building follies with their composition bricks or sitting up in the copper beech tree's maroon chambers, Mr Gordon would sometimes join them. The longer he stayed with his sons the more like them he seemed, although to Mollie the boys did not have the charm of their father, being easy to understand. An indirection in him held him in her thoughts more than she knew, although he looked her in the eyes when he spoke to her, encouraging her to flourish in his difficult gaze.

Rhona Gordon nagged her father, who could not do enough for her. When he made little loaf pans for her and crimped dishes for tartlets out of metal he had pressed and cut himself, she told him, as her mother might have, 'These are sharp for a child, do you not see that?'

The night in the small house was a warm one in late summer. Rhona and Mollie had been awaiting the occasion with a pleasure that had sufficient alarm to it to be interesting. Darkness came at night and who knew what it might contain? Not Germans, after all this time (it was the middle nineteen thirties and the two girls were brought up ostrich fashion), but Englishmen perhaps, over the border for a reiving night? Aged fourteen, the girls were children enough to confuse fear and interest.

No one had told them anything more helpful about these sensations than that the male pigeon is moved, when the mood comes upon him, to 'tread' his mate. A picture of this obscure conjunction did not help. The she pigeon looked compliant, the he pigeon smug. A pointless attention had been paid to the particularities of their plumage, their iridescence, and so on. It was like being shown how to roll an umbrella when what you wanted, if only you knew it, was a voyage in a hot air balloon.

Rhona and Mollie had done their teeth in the farmhouse. They brought out with them a candle and a drum of matches that were not to be used save in an emergency. Through the garden under the waxy trailing leaves of the copper beech, over the rabbit-netting into the fruit cage and out into the orchard's long grass they walked as though they had not been there before ever. Each girl wore a camel dressing gown and carried a stone hot water bottle wrapped in a piece of blanket. They had provisioned the playhouse earlier with apples, bread, butter and splintery-pink rhubarb jam.

Small and burdened the plum trees seemed to gnarl as Mollie walked in the dark between them; they were seemingly changing in shape as though being cooked from beneath, or twisted at the roots. So damp was the grass it was like paddling through wet ribbons as the two approached the playhouse. Mr Gordon had hung a Tilley lamp and shown them earlier in the day how to turn off its light by rolling away the flame.

It was like a cabin inside, warm and close and appointed with no superfluities. The two beds were made up, white as open envelopes.

In bed, the lamp extinguished, the windows opened at a distance nicely judged to take into account both health and marauders, Rhona and Mollie said their prayers and then began to go through the girls in their class, judging who had been kissed. There were seven Fionas in the class so attention had to be paid.

Rhona had not been kissed, in her own opinion, she said. You did not count the Lorimer boy because he did it to everybody. Mollie had not been kissed, although she moaned at her mother's handmirror sometimes and offered her cheek to it, sometimes even her lips. The girls fell asleep after a satisfactory bout of giggling that came to them as a mercy just as they began to talk about ghosts.

In the aware early sleep that leads to dreams, Mollie instructed herself not to talk in her sleep. She did not know what secret she contained, only that one was there. Although Rhona was the talker when they were awake, Mollie spoke out at night and woke herself often at the height of these dreams of puerile adventure and high colour that did not sit naturally with her quiet waking style. When she awoke later, it was neatly, as if she were about to arrive at a station.

She moved out of the cosy bed in two cool movements, casting a glance she realized was duplicitous at her sleeping friend; walked backwards like a sailor down the steps that led to the childish dining set, unlatched the door with the discretion of luck, and went out among the plum trees in her nightdress. Her feet were bare. The trees no longer appeared distorted but ordered in an abundant pattern full of blue, starry all the way down to the shining grass. She took a plum. In the day they were yellow fleshed inside the glowing red skin. By night under combining stars this plum was blue skinned, white fleshed. Although it was not quite ripe and still clung to its stone, she bit it and chewed. A shiny knot of resin had seeped and settled where a wasp had been before her. She wiped the stiff globule off with her thumb and looked up into the face that was higher up than most of the burdensome fruit.

'I woke you with my lamp, did I? Are you cold?' asked Rhona's father, and her absence of fear completed itself.

Sixty years on, after church, Mollie listened to Rhona and watched her as she nagged at the world and set it to rights.

'Would you have done that, though would you, Mollie, I'm asking you, would you ever have been so foolish? Would you not have had the presence of mind to run? Or even to try to do the man some reasonable harm? The good men have gone, the men of honour, the men you could trust, the men like, did you know him, Mollie, my poor father who was wounded in that First War and never the same, so Mother and I, it was hard for us, hard, we had to protect him from his own peculiarities. Of course, I recall now you did meet him. And one night when we slept the night through in my garden house, it was blossom time and the trees were white with the blossom, it made its own light like surf, I'm remembering it now, you said his name in your sleep. You said, "Mr Gordon." It was blossom time, I'll never forget, and we made jeely pieces before it was light. With plum jam. It was a rare night.'

Mollie contrived to maintain the air of uninterest that was the response most familiar to her old, betrayed, dear friend; there was no need at this late stage to look into the roots of the friendship's heartwood, a tired man on a night of nights kissing a young girl next to a deep tank of tar, some days before it came to the time of gathering plums.

AUTUMN IN SOPOT

Gillian Nelson

Witold met the train from Warsaw. Although he bowed to Rachel and kissed her hand, he hardly spoke as they walked down the platform to his car. It was already dark, and raining. He drove to her hotel where he left her with another bow. She had never been to Poland before. The bedroom she was given had a fusty grandeur. Though the basin was boxed in mahogany and had brass taps, there was no plug and the soap, a gritty little tablet, refused to lather or cleanse. When she lay down in the chill bed, she felt the train still moving. This place, long thought of, had seemed unobtainable. Now she was here, it frightened her.

She woke at eight, still afraid, and saw a crack of daylight showing round the velvet curtains. Stepping from rug to rug to avoid the cold floor, she went to the window, drew the cord, lifted the yellowing net – and saw the sea.

Waves in shallow humps were running in sideways and unfurling without foam on the sand. There was nothing between her and this watery field but a strip of grass and a low line of trees. Immediately her tension loosened and she felt free.

Rachel dressed and went outside. Although early, other people were walking quietly along the beach or on the path behind the trees, carrying shopping bags, leading small children. They had rather expressionless faces. She saw the trees were pollarded limes, their damp bark like sealskin. Already, in early November, they were leafless with just a few ochre seed wings hanging on their branches. A horse man in a blue cap came from behind the hotel leading a horse with a striped saddle-cloth. Some swans floated in a group, disdaining the wheeling, scolding seagulls. This was a world remembered from stories of her childhood, and she drew in deep breaths of the salty, seaweedy air.

When she saw Witold coming along the path, her heart sank. She did not want his talk, explanations, interrogations. True, she had come for that; already did not want it.

Her cousin was wearing a grey overcoat, like felted armour. He greeted her gravely. A brown beret settled firmly over his domed head allowed no hair to show, so accentuated the long lines of his face, the shape of his skull. He looked ready for their encounter.

'Sleep well?' he enquired courteously. 'It is to be hoped you did.'

'Deeply anyway.'

'Shall we go into the hotel?'

'I'd rather be outdoors.'

He frowned but she had already turned back to face the sea.

'Very well then.' His tone was one of disapproval laced with patience.

As they began to stroll along, he made the sort of remarks he had avoided the night before.

'So, what were your impressions of Warsaw?'

Rachel said brightly, 'Poland seems altogether more buoyant than I'd expected from the newspapers in Britain.'

Her cousin did not appear pleased to hear this. His face, which was colourless, deeply grooved, with sculpted lips, was severe and so shadowed it was like dusty ivory.

'Hard days will return,' he told her. 'And not just here. Across all Europe.'

'I hope not. It does feel cheerful, you know, in a subdued sort of way.'

He raised his thin eyebrows, and they walked on in silence. The beach was on the right-hand side of the path and on the left were square houses with verandahs, houses set back in gardens.

'And is Sopot how you imagined?' Witold tried.

'Not at all. I hadn't thought of the sea.'

'But that's crazy.' For the first time his voice sounded unconstrained. 'The whole point of the place is that it's a seaside spa.'

'I just hadn't thought of his life happening beside the sea.'

'Does that make such a difference?'

'It would for most people! If the sea is there it alters the land. The swans too – the romance of them.'

'Are swans romantic? Commonplace and rather spiteful, I'd have said.'

The birds had come to the water's edge where a child and her mother had crusts to throw. The woman was wrapped in a drab fur, but the child wore an evidently new coat and a fleecy hood framed her face that was alight with the pleasure and the scariness of being so near the large, feathered creatures. One of them came splashing out on splayed feet. Two other children ran up, excited and nervous too, holding out scraps of bread and then, as the swan came close, throwing them down and retreating with tiny shrieks of laughter.

'What pretty kids,' said Rachel.

Witold smiled grimly. 'Soon they'll be as dull and trapped as their parents are.'

His sourness repelled Rachel, and, as they walked on, she tried to ignore him, for she wanted to like this place, to enter it. She even hoped for what had seemed impossible, to be happy here.

The horizon was clear and distant, an inked line below which merchant shipping was passing in slow procession in and out of Gdansk; yet on the land there was an autumnal mist and the path with its limetrees faded into greyness half a mile away. The horseman had trotted off into this distance.

'It is like a dream,' said Rachel, half to herself.

'I would have thought that for you it would be a nightmare.' Again his voice jolted her.

'It has been but now . . . it's uncanny, as if an illustration in a storybook had come to life. Something from Grimm – the cold, northern shore, the swans on the sea – something you don't see at home – and the rider on the sands.'

'I do not understand you at all, Rachel.' He banged his feet down as loudly as he could on the pebbled path. 'You badger me for months to tell you exactly what happened, you say it will tame your demons, help you to be fully well. And now – such talk!'

She was as irritating as her letters had been, her many letters, none showing sufficient courtesy or self-control. He supposed that the British, never having had to come nose to nose, eye to eye with such desperate reality as his countrymen, had not learned the good manners, the dignity, that tragedy demands. In the end, after months of entreaty, he had told her the stark fact: her father had betrayed her Jewish mother to the SS.

'But you were not appeased,' he told her now. 'You started agitating again, to come here, to see. See what, I ask. But I agree. You come. You are here, and indulging in fancy talk of fairy tales.'

She took his arm, which he yielded unwillingly. 'Yes, thank you for telling me. It was hard for you, I know, to reopen all that.' No response. 'I am sure I did thank you. Not at first. It was such a dreadful shock. I couldn't even think about it. I just buried it.' She was not looking at Witold but at the sea as if it could offer comfort, or an answer. Though calm, the sea's entire surface was just perceptibly puckered by the wind, like a wincing skin. 'Once when I was a child I was taken to see a medieval church, in England somewhere, that had wall paintings of the harrowing of hell, you know? Naked, writhing bodies, demon faces lit by flames, pitchforks, people upside down with burning hair. I let that stand for what my mother suffered.'

'Near enough,' said Witold stolidly.

'But not real. When I did let myself think, I found I was asking myself about him, not her. How and why he did it. I thought the place where he lived might give me an answer. How could a man hand his wife over to save a hotel?'

'He lost that too, of course. The Nazis turned it into a sort of officers' club and Stefan just took orders from them, became a menial, harried, jumped on, terrified.'

'Is the hotel still here?'

'No, the Russians destroyed it, but it was like these that remain, though larger and more luxurious. Smart, you could say.' He had gestured with his head, nodding his beret in the direction of the small hotels and large villas beside the path. In their gardens were wooden benches, pieces of statuary, gravel walks through small shrubberies. Yellowing leaves were everywhere – on the trees, on the ground, drifting from the trees and catching on gutters, and seats, and the flat tops of clipped hedges. Weak sunlight, filtering through the mist, lit up the gardens and the glassed verandahs that jutted towards the sea. Momentarily, the place regained its air of leisure and pleasure, of idleness and timelessness.

Witold said, 'Our grandfather, the first Stefan, opened the Hotel Flore in the nineties at the time the pier was built. In old postcards the two appear together. If you were anyone at all you stayed at the Hotel Flore, took the waters in the Pump Room, were photographed on the pier in your Parisian outfit, and lost money at Stefan's casino after the excellent dinner he also provided. Between the wars your father, the second Stefan, was, one could say, the King of Sopot.'

'You mean he took his place in some sort of comedy of manners.' Rachel found the idea not unpleasing.

'He was handsome and women were wild about him it's said, but he had little interest in them. He didn't marry for years, just worked flat out at his businesses, the hotel primarily and the casino, but he owned a string of dress shops too.'

'He must have had some relaxation.'

'I'm told he went to Hel sometimes.'

'He cracked up?'

Witold snorted with harsh laughter. 'Not he! Hel is a place.'

'I know. I've been there.'

'It's a place up the coast. Hel with one "l". He used to take odd days off up there, to fish and paint. He thought he had some talent as an artist. Hel's a port at the end of a spit of sand and pine trees.'

Rachel was offended that Witold should tease her in this humourless way, and pulled her arm away. Hell for her was the mental hospital and before.

Workmen had been sweeping fallen leaves into piles and now set fire to them. An acid smell of burning mingled with those of seaweed, moist grass, damp sand. Every hundred yards a gap in the trees gave a view of the beach scattered with walkers, and the sea which was now green-blue with the sun on it. The only sounds were the scratch of brooms, footfalls, the occasional cry of bird or child, and the whooshing murmur of the waves.

'It is hard to credit cruelty and betrayal,' said Rachel, 'here.'

'My God! This place is rotten with it. Not just torturing Jews, most as harmless as your mother. The Germans mauling the Poles, then the Russians turning their attentions to us. Even Poles crucifying Poles. Remember the massacres at the shipyards? Over there.' He jabbed a thumb eastwards along the shore to the blot of cranes and derricks that was Gdansk. 'And back in history, waves of invaders, barbarians, Huns, murdering knights. Poland is bloodsoaked, Rachel.' As he spoke the grooves on either side of his long, thin mouth deepened. They looked like cuts. 'We cannot expect anything else.'

'You are terribly disillusioned.'

'Yes,' he agreed, not a whit put out. 'The only adult response to life is either loss of illusion or madness.'

A surprised laugh was forced out of her. 'Well, as one who opted for the madhouse – '

'You are cured.' He turned to her with concern. 'You must believe that.'

'Coming here was to be part of my cure.'

The swans came floating into view again, wavelets splashing on their pillow-like breasts. Rachel thought of the story of the seven princes changed into swans and their sister weaving shirts of rushes for them, sewing with thorn needles that tore her fingers. In the end she did release her brothers from the spell.

As if in mocking comment, from the town behind came the klaxon of a train, then the rumble and clank of wagons passing over the bridge. Cattle trucks had taken the Jews to the camps. No release for her mother, no love working magic.

These were old thoughts. She slumped against Witold.

'What's the matter? Are you ill?'

'I want to be free.'

'Yes, that's what your father wanted – to be free of love's stranglehold. He took a wife for comfort, amusement and decoration, but didn't want her when she meant trouble.' He looked at Rachel. 'You are very pale.'

'I think I'm hungry. I didn't have any breakfast, wanting to be by the sea, or anything last night on the train.'

He looked ready to censure her, but merely said, 'We can get something in the Grand Hotel, past the pier.'

It was a massive place with sloping concrete ramps and here the lawns were swept clear of all leaves. It was still not ten o'clock and breakfast was being served in a barn-like dining room. At the door two waitresses seated on chairs handed them each a ticket which entitled them to a choice from a buffet table. They could select eggs, hot or cold, boiled sausages, salami, liver sausage, ham, and with that rolls, croissants, jam, honey, pastes, weak coffee, watery tea, or boiled milk in tall tumblers too hot to hold unless you wrapped them in a paper napkin made of such thin, shiny paper that they slipped. Everyone present was eating heartily. Rachel did not enjoy the taste of anything she tried. There was a bitterness in her mouth.

'What was my mother like, Witold?'

'Suzi? Quite a silly and selfish young woman.'

'How can you say that!'

'How? Well, it's a fact and you asked.' (Again this British un-wish to face the bare truth.) 'She was always wanting money for luxuries and lived on Stefan's indulgence. He met her in his dress shop where she was briefly an assistant. Very pretty and appealing, like a kitten. Flirtatious, and unfaithful.'

'You make it sound novelettish,' she said coldly. She stared out of the window which looked towards the town. There were few people about.

'When hard times came she expected Stefan to smooth things out. Suzi reproached, wept, was indiscreet. Hotel-keepers fear indiscretion like the plague.'

'All of which, even if true, does not justify –'

'What could? Can anything, ever, excuse a betrayal. No; not even of the weakest trust. Isn't it the worst thing?'

Rachel sipped the scalding milk. She swallowed a piece of flabby croissant, her eyes on the pale, sad, stern face of her cousin. She considered various responses. 'Yes, the very worst,' she said.

'At least Stefan had you smuggled away, in a hotel laundry basket it is said in the family. He is supposed to have tried to persuade Suzi to go, but she was not the sort who could have faced a long, dangerous journey alone.'

'But let me be despatched into the unknown.'

'She wasn't cut out for motherhood, from what I've heard.'

'From what you've heard. Poor mother.'

Rachel's emotions were veering; and she was not entirely

unwilling to hear what Witold was telling her. The idea of her mother's fate had kept her in a prison for years. It was a release of a sort to hear of her father, if not good, then at least fairness.

'He tried to get you back after the war.'

'Yes. But my adopted parents thought, I came to agree, it never . . . We never imagined then that the old life could catch up with me.'

Witold thought this one of the more unrealistic of her opinions, but said nothing. There was silence while he ate and she looked out of the window. A tram slid into view, stopped, let passengers off and on, moved away.

'I thought Sopot would be a terrible place, but it's settled and calm, rather melancholy.'

'Not for long.' He was digging the yolk out of a boiled egg, his second.

'You *do* look for the dark side.'

'We Poles live in the shadows.'

'I don't. I am a Pole too.'

Witold looked up from his plate and stared directly at her for the first time since she had stepped off the train. He searched her face with a penetrating, shrewd gaze. 'You have become British. They have virtues, but lack ours – despairing courage and pessimism.'

'Is pessimism a virtue?'

He made no reply. He saw no point. She could never understand.

When they went outside, Witold led her to the pier and showed her the pre-war postcards now re-issued. How ironic, she thought, that these remained and were bringing in a profit while all the people had been swept away. She bought a couple.

In their blue-and-white, sea-and-sky brightness nothing in Sopot was other than clean, gay and attractive. They showed throngs of holiday-makers elaborately dressed in the style of the time, the men in straw boaters, the little girls in long white socks and frilled skirts, the women with feather-edged parasols. Strings of coloured flags were looped between the lamp posts on the pier. Rachel wished profoundly that she could slip into this world that she held in her wool-gloved hand and stay there, the future unobtainable.

Witold took the cards and put them in his breast pocket, then rebuttoned his overcoat and adjusted his scarf. They walked on towards a pavilion with an octagonal roof, red-tiled and topped by a copper lantern. The corners of this building were set with towers, each with a cupola and graceful pinnacle. The white paintwork was fresh, and pink sandstones picked out the elegant windows. Being so near the shore, the pavilion stood up against the sky, very bold and enticing.

'What is it, Witold?'

'A physiotherapy place, I think. Some government health centre, at any rate. It was the Pump Room.'

'Oh, do let's go in. It's sure to be pretty inside.'

'I think not,' he said, but she had already run to the door so he followed, irritated afresh by unthinkingness.

Through the outer door Rachel found a flight of steps leading upwards to a second door with copper handles, in the form of fishes. She grasped one in each hand and pushed. Immediately inside a striped woollen curtain hung from a semi-circular rail. More timidly, she parted this with her hands.

The room is square under its octagonal roof. There are dolphins carved on the cornices, and tiles painted with ferns and waves. Once it was a charming place for casual meetings, now it is a waiting room smelling faintly of wet clothing, crowded with patients, weary and forlorn. The dolphins are painted a sickly yellow and curtains shroud the tiles. A woman wearing an apron stands behind a counter selling a few nothings – hair-setting lotion, socks, comics. Another woman will take your coat and give you a ticket. She is knitting with some violet wool. There is a strip of worn carpet on the floor covering the mosaic of Poseidon.

'It was here,' said Witold with sudden resolution, 'that the Jews who had been rounded up were kept until the trains came for them.'

'Oh no!'

'Terrified, their bowels loose with terror, hardly able to breathe, let alone move, for the numbers packed in. Some were dead when the doors were eventually opened, crushed and suffocated. They were lucky, one must say. The corpses near the door tumbled down those steps you ran up.'

'Please don't.'

'What did you come for then?' he asked roughly.

His voice was disturbing the waiting people. Although they could not hear what this man was saying to the woman who stood, half leaning against him, they probably knew well enough what it was about this place that would make a woman feel faint. The attendant put down her knitting, came across to suggest to Witold that he either sit down, or leave.

The day was colder, the mist thicker and the smoke from the fires denser, mingling with the mist and drifting over the beach.

'Why did you do that? Let me go in there and then tell me. It was too cruel.' She was panting and very pale.

'You came to see for yourself, didn't you? See and understand? But you can't. No one can really know how it was.'

She continued to stare bitterly at him, which made him uneasy so he guided her to a bench in an alcove of bushes. She was unwilling to sit, and cold. She pulled her feet on to the seat and wrapped her skirt and coat round her legs. Then he said to her,

'Suzi was one of the women who died in there. She never went anywhere else, Rachel.'

She seized his shoulders as if to shake him in fury, then

was arrested and kept still, looking at his face, pale, controlled, lifeless.

'There were no cattle trucks for your mother, no gas chamber. It was a relatively quick death by suffocation and terror.'

Listlessly, she dropped her hands and faced the sea again. She began to cry without a sound, the tears slipping one after another down her cheeks and dripping off her jaw on to her coat collar.

She cried with the effort to understand and with the knowledge that she never could. She cried for herself, the years of agony built on the wrong facts.

She had wept for Suzi many times. Perhaps this was to be the last.

After a while she stopped, and Witold handed her a clean, folded handkerchief. She kept her face averted from him and fixed her eyes on the sea, which comforted her in its familiar way. Slowly her breathing calmed. Her fit of weeping changed nothing.

It occurred to her that she had come to Sopot in part because she wished to forgive her father. If so, she had failed. You could not forgive the dead, or blame them. They were not there.

The horse they had seen earlier came by at a gallop, horse and man straining forward and kicking backwards clods of wet sand, which flew up and dropped back like wounded birds.

'Your father used to ride here early in the morning before the day at the hotel began. He prized exercise, fitness.'

A girl walking on the beach waved and the rider checked his horse. She stroked the beast's nose, and the man leant down to her. Her skirt, his jacket, the water behind were all the same faded denim. This place, Rachel thought, is weary of its past.

She saw Witold was looking at her as if wanting a response.

'Do you remember my father?'

'Yes. He didn't die until the sixties.'

'Even though he was a known collaborator?'

'His type survives.'

What type is that, she wondered. Except for one shocking and dreadful act of death, her father sounded not unlike herself – solitary, hardworking, not especially interested in sex, loving the sea and its spread loneliness. Could a seed of such treachery be lurking in her, waiting its chance? Certainly she was a survivor. Here she was, after all, fit and well, with a good job and even friends, after all those dreadful years. But then, it stands to reason, everyone who is out here in the world has survived, at least this far. Even some Jews survived the camps.

'I used to think,' she said to Witold, reestablishing contact with him, 'think or dream, fear really, that my mother had not died in the camp and that, if I searched diligently enough, I'd find her.'

'Oh.' He was not interested in fantasy.

'I used to have plans to search for her in refuges for old, lost women: yet I dreaded she might repulse me if I found her. I look like Stefan, after all.'

Witold was silent. Since he had told her what had actually happened to Suzi, there was no point in pursing these ideas. Rachel clearly wanted to go on. He sighed inwardly, and reminded himself that she would soon return to Britain where she could settle back into the nostalgic introspection and naive optimism that seemed to go hand-in-hand there. She was still talking.

'Doesn't the very thought of it shrivel you up? The not knowing, the barest possibility that she could be alive still in some sordid dump, used to drive me mad. I mean, literally, it did.'

He took her hand in both of his. He wanted to be kind to his cousin.

'But life is uncertainty, Rachel, and fear of loss, and loss itself. Who avoids it? And should we wish to, since it is a part of our humanity.'

As he spoke he was staring bleakly at the Baltic Sea. The swans had floated farther out and were strung in a line. A mile or more beyond them a ship was moving off to the west, and from the north a bank of cloud was piling on the horizon.

THE UNTHINKABLE HAPPENS TO PEOPLE EVERY DAY

Ali Smith

I'm sorry son but there's no one of that name lives here.

The man hung up, stood in the phone box and breathed out slowly. Without warning London surrounded him, widening round him like rings in water with its scruffy paintpeeled shops, its streets leading into other insignificant streets, its anonymous houses for all the grey seeable distance. Someone rapped on the glass, a woman scowling from under her umbrella, and as he came out he saw people waiting in a line behind her. He crossed the road and stood outside a television shop with the sets in the windows showing one of the daytime programmes where two presenters and an expert discuss an issue and viewers phone in and talk about it. That was when he went inside the shop and within a few minutes had smashed several of the sets.

Now the man was driving too fast for his car, he could hear it rattling and straining under the tape of The Corries, the one tape that had been in the glove compartment when he looked. Above the noise there was a hum in his ears like when you wet your finger and run it round the rim of a glass. He thought that's what it had been like, like going into a room full of wine glasses. Nothing but wine glasses from one end of the floor to the other, imagine. As soon as you got into a room like that, he thought, the temptation to kick would be too strong. The same as when he was a boy and they visited the McGuinness's, when he was handed that china saucer and the cup with the fragile handle, with the lip of it so thin against his own that it would be really easy to bite through. As soon as a thought like that came into your head you wanted to try it. That ache in his arm to twitch suddenly and send the tea into the air. That would have made his folks laugh. They might have been cross to start with, but after that it'd have been something to remember.

He had stepped inside the TV shop to get out of the way of passers-by. Sleek new televisions were ranged in front of him, small ones on the top shelf, larger ones on the middle, massive wide-screen sets on the floor on metal stands. All except two were showing the same picture and the sound was turned up on one; he heard the presenter hurrying a caller off the air so as to bring the next person on. The woman he was hurrying had apparently just told them about a wasting disease her daughter aged nineteen had been diagnosed as having and the bespectacled expert, presumably a doctor giving advice, was shaking his head dolefully at the camera. The presenter said, well thank you for that call Yvonne, we hope we've brought a little bit of comfort to you on that, and your daughter too, but now let's go over to Tom who's calling from Coventry, I believe he's just heard he's been found HIV positive, am I right, Tom? The maps on the screens flashed where Coventry was.

The man leaned forward and tipped the television in front of him off its shelf; it crashed onto the top of the television below it. Its screen fragmented and there was a small explosion as all the sets in the shop went blank. In the time it took the young woman serving another man in the video section to get to the door of the shop, he had launched a portable cassette radio through the screen of another set and sent a line of small televisions chained together hurtling one after the other simply by nudging the first.

I'm sorry, it couldn't be helped, was what the man said.

The woman told her boss, Mr Brewer, this, and that before she had a chance to call for help or anything he was off and because she was so shocked she didn't see which way. What the woman didn't tell Mr Brewer was that actually the man had stood in the debris before he left and had slowly and carefully written down an address and a telephone number on one of the price display cards as he apologized. She had the piece of card folded in her back pocket and could feel it pressing against her as she spoke to Mr Brewer. Maybe the man hadn't given her his real address. That was something she didn't want to know. Maybe he had, though. That was what she didn't want Mr Brewer to know.

Side two of The Corries ended again and the machine switched automatically back over to side one. The last sign had flashed past before he'd had a chance to see where he was. In the middle years of his life, in the middle of a dark wood. He couldn't remember what that was from. In the middle lane of the motorway in the middle of the night. In a service station in the middle of nowhere in the middle of a cigarette. He held his coffee and stared out into the dark. He ought to phone his wife, they'd maybe be frantic. Or perhaps he could try the number again. There were three payphones by the exit. Think about just picking up the receiver, putting the coin in, pressing the number he knew the shape of like he knew the shape of his own hands, the telephone ringing there in the dark. But look at the time, he didn't want to wake anybody, that wouldn't do, and so he drained his coffee and headed back to the car.

At first light the road was so full of steep drops and sudden lifts that it was like being at sea; he had to travel most of it in second gear. It was light enough to read the word SCOTLAND on the big rock as he passed. The Corries snapped near Pitlochry in the middle of the Skye Boat Song. Since Scotland is only a few hours long, it was about ten when he tried the number again, this time from a call box in sight of the house. He lifted the receiver and pressed the numbers; he closed his eyes tightly and opened them again to try to get rid of the dizzy feeling. The garden, the walls, the door. The tree, much bigger. The lawn, the hedge. The next door. The whole block. The sky above it. The bus shelter, the grass where the bus shelter met the concrete, the little cracks in the edges of the kerb, different, the same. The same, but new houses had been built at the back where the field had been. The windows of the new houses, with their different kinds and colours of curtains. Even before the phone was answered, he knew.

No, I'm sorry. Look, is it not you that's phoned a few times already? I'm sorry, I can't help you there son. There's nobody of that name here.

I know, he said. I won't call again. I'm really sorry to have bothered you. I'm just being stupid.

After that it was random. Soon he was coasting the wet green carsick roads of the north; a little later he saw that the petrol he had bought in Edinburgh was almost gone. His car eventually ground to a halt on a gravelly back road next to a small loch. The man wound down the window and as the sound of his car in his ears died away he heard water and birds. He opened the door and stood up. Further down the beach a child was crouched like a frog on the stones, her hair hanging; behind her was a big white-painted house converted into a roadside restaurant, closed for the season. A pockmarked sign on the roof of the house said HIELAN HAME, underneath, in smaller letters, BURGERS BAR-B-Q TRADITIONAL SCOTTISH FARE LICENSED. Behind this a mass of trees, behind them in the distance two mountains still with snow on the peaks, then the sky, empty.

The man walked across the stones and stood in the litter at the edge of the water. The car door hung open behind him, and the engine clicked as it cooled down. A bird sang in the grey air. Water seeped cold over the sides of his shoes.

*

It was the Easter holidays and the girl was out on the stones looking for insects or good skimmers. Sometimes if you turned a big stone over you could find slaters underneath, it depended how close to the water it was. The real name for slaters was woodlice. The girl had decided to collect insects for various experiments. She wanted to try racing them, she also wanted to try putting different kinds in a Tupperware box together and to see which kinds survived when you left them in water. Last summer she had discovered tiny tunnels in the back garden and she had followed one to an ant colony in the manure heap. To see what would happen she had poured Domestos from the kitchen cupboard onto it. First a white scum had come and some ants had writhed in it taking a long time to die. The others had gone mad, running in all directions, some carrying white egg-looking things bigger than themselves. They had set up another colony on the other side of the heap and for days she had watched them cleaning out their old place, lines of ants carrying the dead bodies away and leaving them in neat piles under one of the rosebushes. She was very sorry she had done that thing. This year she was going to be more scientific but kind as well, except to wasps. If they were stupid enough to go in the jam-jars and drown it was their own fault.

Here was a good flat stone. As she stood up to see how many skims it would have she saw the man who had left his car in the middle of the road walking into the loch. He sat down in the water about ten feet out. Then his top half fell backwards and he disappeared.

She ran along the bay to look for him; she heard a splash somewhere behind her and turned round. The man was sitting up in the water again. He looked about the same age as her uncle, and she watched him take some things out of his pocket and fiddle about with them. As she got closer she saw he was trying to light a wet cigarette.

Mister, excuse me, she said, but your car's in the middle of the road, people can't get by.

The man shook his hand away from himself so he wouldn't drip water down onto a match.

Excuse me, mister, but is it not a bit cold, the water? Anyway your matches are soaking – my mother's got a lighter. I know where it's kept.

The man looked embarrassed. He pulled himself to his feet unsteadily and wiped his hair back off his face, then stumbled back through the shallows. The girl watched the water running off him. She didn't know whether to call him mister or sir.

Are you drunk, sir?

No, I'm not drunk, the man said, smiling. Water from his clothes darkened the stones. How old are you then? he asked.

The girl kept her distance. I'm nine, she said. My mother says I'm not to talk to strangers.

Your mother's quite right. I've got a daughter your age. Her name's Fiona, the man said, looking at his feet and shivering.

I told you it was cold, said the girl. She twisted round to skim her stone.

I could show you how to skim stones, said the man.

I know how to skim stones, the girl said, giving him her most scornful look. She expertly pitched the stone against the surface of the loch. The man scrabbled about at his feet to find himself a good stone and she stepped out of the range of the drips that flew off him when he threw.

Not as good as you, said the man. You're an expert right enough.

That's because I do it every day, said the girl so the man wouldn't feel too bad. I live here, so I can. Are you on holiday here? Where do you live? she asked.

47

The man went a funny colour. Then he said, well when I was your age I used to live not far from here. You don't sound very Scottish, said the girl. That's because I've lived in London for a long time, said the man. The girl said she'd like to live in London, she'd been there once and seen all the places they show you on TV. When she grew up, she wanted to work for TV, maybe on programmes about animals. Then she asked the man did he know that Terry Wogan owned all those trees over there. Does he? said the man. Yes, and a Japanese man whose name she couldn't remember owned the land over there behind the loch. Who owns the loch? the man asked. Me, I do, said the girl. And my father owns the house and my mother runs the restaurant. Are you redundant? My uncle was made redundant.

The man told the girl that no, he wasn't redundant and that, believe it or not, he worked for television. Had she ever heard of the programme called *The Unthinkable Happens to People Every Day*? The girl said she thought her mother watched it. Then she said suspiciously, I don't recognize you from off the TV.

No, said the man, I'm not *on* the TV. I work in the background. I do things like phone up the people who write to us and ask them to come on the show to talk about the unthinkable thing that's happened to them. Then I add up how much it'll cost for them to come, and decide how long they'll get to talk about it.

The girl had grown respectful and faintly excited about talking to someone who might work for TV. She couldn't tell whether the water running down the man's face was from his eyes or his hair. He looked very sad and she suddenly felt sorry for him even though he wasn't actually redundant. She decided to do something about it.

Would you like to come up onto the roof? she asked the man.

Would I what? he said.

Would you like to come up onto the roof and throw some stones? I know this really easy way to get up there, said the girl.

The man filled his wet jacket pockets with stones the girl selected. She showed him, springing up lightly, how to climb from the coalshed roof onto the extension. From there the man could heave himself after her up the drainpipe.

You have to be very quiet or my mother'll hear, said the girl. It's a wonderful view even on a day like today, isn't it?

Yes, the man whispered.

The girl pointed at the HIELAN HAME sign twenty feet away. She was obviously a good shot; the paint had been chipped in hundreds of small dents.

It's two points for big letters and five points for small ones. There's a special bonus if you can hit the c of Scottish, she said. But *your* arms are probably long enough so that you could even reach the loch from here if you wanted, she added hopefully.

Right, said the man. Taking a stone as big as his palm, he hurled it. They watched it soar in silence, then there was a distant splash as it hit the water.

Yes! cried the girl. Yes! You did it! Nobody's ever done that before! Nobody ever reached the loch before! She jumped up and down. The man looked surprised and then very pleased.

Anne-Marie! called her mother at the thumping. Anne-Marie, I've *told* you about that roof. Now get down here. If you're at that sign again you'll feel the back of my hand.

The girl led the man down off the roof, watching that he put his feet in all the right places. Her mother, angry at first at a stranger being up on her roof, was soon amazed and delighted to meet someone who worked on *The Unthinkable Happens to People Every Day*. She made him tea and a salad, apologizing for the fact that the restaurant was closed and there wasn't anything grander, and she dried his suit off for him. He told her that he was sort of a local boy really, but that he'd lived in England for a while. She said she could spot it in his accent. Had he been up visiting his parents, then? No, they were both dead, both some years ago now. He'd been up for a drive and to look at the place again. She asked him how he'd got wet. He said he'd fallen into the loch. He filled his car from a tank of petrol in the garage and before he left he promised the girl that he'd get the autographs of some famous children's TV presenters for her when he got back to work.

Some weeks later a packet arrived addressed to the Hielan Hame. Inside was a thank you letter for the girl's mother and several photographs of celebrities all signed To Ann Marie with best wishes. The girl took them to school and showed them to all her friends. She didn't even mind that they'd spelled her name wrong.

These are from the man who hit the loch, she told her friends. He works for the TV and he's been up on our roof.

THE STRANGE MARRIAGE
OF ALBERT EINSTEIN AND
PHILIPP LENARD

G. W. Fraser

Lately, when the drink is in me, and our old house creaks in the winter darkness, I find myself bawling upstairs to their cold, empty rooms, to come down to the warmth and hear the philosopher.

Listen, children, and don't be afraid, and come and sit with your demented father. And he will tell you all there is to know, about dismal sciences and Love and Physics.

First question: who made the modern world?

She said Bertrand Russell did, in between rain showers on a spring day in Bloomsbury.

In this, as in so many things, Francesca was wrong. The world did not spring as she thought it should have, from the logical philosophy of good and kind men. It was mostly invented between the years 1890 and 1930, in primitive apparatus of sealing wax and string, in a small number of ramshackle laboratories in England and in the Kaiser's Germany; in Manchester and Cambridge and in Heidelberg, where, in the year 1895, the son of a Bratislavan wine merchant, Philipp Edward Anton Lenard, shone pure beams of light on polished metals.

First confession: I've never seen a portrait of Philipp Edward Anton Lenard. I have this satisfactory stereotype in my mind's eye, all broken veins and Mittel Europa. He wears a huge black coat and a wing collar and carries too much beard and when he frowns, which is often, his brow is crossed by lines like irrigation ditches. His mother died when he was a small boy and his father immediately married his aunt. So, in my likeness of Philipp Lenard, there is no forgiveness. He has the face of a judge. The father, the sisters, Humanity and God Himself; the criminals of Lenard's boyhood are all on trial. When he tires of the judicial process and they are finally condemned, he will hang them himself.

Philipp Lenard was a difficult man. He delighted in difficult measurements. His observations of metals and light confounded, in subtle ways, the great theories of physics which then held sway.

Second question: What is light, apart from God?
Philipp Lenard had measured a part of the answer.

Philipp Lenard, like light, had a dual nature. In 1905, he became the fifth man, and the second German, to receive the Nobel prize for Physics, for his momentous experiments with the *Kathodenstrahlen* – the Cathode rays, the electrons. But, by then, he had also quarrelled with the great Heinrich Hertz, his former professor and one-time mentor. Hertz's father's family were Jews. He had begun a feud with John Joseph Thomson about whether he, Lenard, or the Cambridge man, had made certain important discoveries first. He had begun to complain that the British were systematically plagiarizing the work of Aryan science.

And then an obscure clerk in the patent office in Berne, the one young Jew that everyone knows, published a paper with a pompous title: 'On a heuristic viewpoint concerning the production and transformation of light,' and stole Lenard's great glory away. With two bold assumptions and a single equation, Albert Einstein explained all the puzzles of Lenard's light and metals and turned his Physics upside-down.

Thus a jealous marriage was contracted, a marriage

between incompatibles, between the experimenter and the theorist, between the anti-Semite and the Jew, between the fearsome pedant and the joker, and the precious child they raised was called the quantum.

Wherever it was that she met me, I met her at a Festival party, on a rainy August night in the Lawnmarket. She had made her reputation that same spring, with a book of short stories called *The Radio Ophelia*. She was up from London with her last senior citizen, a fashionable Cambridge historian with the improbable vowel sounds of an old cement mixer. His period was the nineteen thirties. Sir Oswald Muesli and the East End marches.

If she were telling this story, our eyes would meet in the usual fashion, across the smoky space of a crowded room. I find her stories always tend to banality. She'd forget that we were both twenty-eight years old, and, in our contrasting ways, each as pretentious as the other. She chain-smoked Gauloises and wore no make-up and I quoted John Donne in my every seduction. Thus, in that crowded room:

> Our eye beams twisted and did thread
> Our eyes upon one double string.

We fell into bed with the inevitability of moons falling in the gravity of a neutron star. In our hard collision, a strange thing happened. We made each other virgins again. We made each other shy and clumsy. We made each other smile. I made a fool of History and Francesca laughed and laughed till her high cheeks were sore.

I told her I loved her as rigorously as I could. She expected rigour in a scientist. I told her I loved her four times:

> Once for each of Nature's forces
> Once for each of Maxwell's Laws
> Once for each of Life's four bases
> Twice in anger, twice in awe.

Now the falling moons are shattered. They cannot even agree the time and the place of their first coalescence. She says we first met in the National Gallery, on the Castle Mound, the Monday after the Lawnmarket party. She says there never was an English historian, and if there was, he had the diction of an angel. She claims to recall the day's *Scotsman* headline; the time and the temperature and the relative humidity; the dollar-yen rate and the Nikkei Stock Index. She remembers all the portraits and their catalogue numbers and, above all, the look of scientific lust that was on my face.

In nineteen nineteen, with Germany in ruins, British eclipse expeditions to the tropics brought back the news that Einstein's General Theory of Relativity, developed in Berlin during the Great War, was true. Space and Time were no more absolutes than the might of the Kaiser's army. The British had captured the Sun and the stars. There was nothing left in Weimar for a patriot to cling on to.

In September nineteen twenty, the German Physical Society, the Naturforscher Gesellschaft, met in the Badehaus in the spa town of Bad Neuheim, near Frankfurt. The young Jew was by then the most famous scientist in the world, and, in certain quarters, the most reviled. The sober citizens of Bad Neuheim woke to find their conference hall ringed by police armed with fixed bayonets.

Lenard speaks first for the Anti-Relativity Company. I see him standing up slowly in his great black coat, his hands clutching his lapels, and speaking with the immense prestige, the absolute gravitas of the Nobel laureate. A sheaf of notes lie open on the lectern. He ignores them. He composes his judge's face. He does not look directly at Einstein. He says, almost with regret, that the simple understanding of the scientist must take exception to Einstein's theory. Observations, yes; equations, no.

The boy Einstein makes a joke to his neighbour. It is certainly a joke at the buffoon's expense. Then

Einstein replies: and what, he asks, have the British observed? The bending of starlight in the gravitational field of the Sun, by precisely the amount predicted in his equations.

For Einstein, the success of the British expedition has clearly settled all arguments, but Lenard, my Lenard, is no longer listening: the purity of noble Aryan science must be protected from contamination by dogmatic Jewish theory. His hands, metaphorically, rise to cover his ears. He shakes his head. He looks at Einstein in exasperation. I can sense he is about to explode with rage, but a strange sort of love is holding him back.

With the rambling intercessions of various minor professors, the conference session on relativity draws peacefully to a close. Ehrenfest, its beleaguered chairman, breathes a sigh of relief and the armed forces of Weimar sheath up their bayonets.

For all the hatred I feel for her now, I have to admit that she once was lovely. The beauty was all Italian, from her father-the-deserter's side. In all our years together, she never talked about her father, but she kept a secret photograph of him in a box on her dressing table. She took it out occasionally when our sons were growing, to look for likenesses.

The photograph had been taken on a farm in Morayshire in December nineteen forty-four. Her father's arms were round two pretty land girls. There was frost on the ground. His POW's uniform was much too big, but his feckless grin was bigger still. He had learned to smile in Ravenna, where a sun shines that never shines on Moray. I expect he was smiling still, when, ten years later, he suddenly left his Scots wife and four-month-old daughter and buggered off back there.

Third question: who could be proud of such a man?

*   *   *

Francesca diligently spread rumours of a Contessa among her great-aunts, or at least the tragic mistress of a Count. She showed me another picture once, of a young woman in a white dress who looked just like her, taken among nobility on the island of Capri in the summer of nineteen twenty-four, not long after the *fascisti* had marched upon Rome.

Her thin face became the more striking, the more she left it unadorned. She wore her femininity entirely about her ears, as earnest young women always used to do, in dabs of French scent and large golden earrings. Her hair was long and black. Her eyes were brown. You could see the anger rising in them a long way off, like a tornado in the distance on the great plains of Kansas.

I suppose I was always frightened of her.

I suppose I always secretly acknowledged the poisonous dullness of my own methodical soul and saw her as the antidote.

I never moved the bed around, except with her. When we were two years married and she was desperate for children, she read that making love with straight backs, with your spines aligned to the magnetic field of the earth, maximized your chances of healthy children.

I never heard lullabies sung, like the ones she sang to our north-south babies. When we fought, late at night, and the boys woke up crying, then she'd lull them back to sleep with folk songs and hymn tunes. She sang 'What a friend we have in Jesus', with lyrics she'd amended:

> Who, I wonder, is your father?
> Little baby bunting mine
> Not that snoring, boring ruin
> But somebody wild and fine

In nineteen twenty-two, the Swedish Academy awarded Einstein the Nobel prize for Physics 'especially for the discovery of the law of the photoelectric effect' – the law of light and metals. Lenard's complaint to Stockholm was bitter and immediate. He accused the Swedes of sanctioning the unproven Jewish relativity by honouring its founder for other things.

That same year, Walter Rathenau, the Minister of Foreign Affairs in the Weimar Government, was assassinated by right-wing extremists outside his home in the Berlin Grünewald. An official day of mourning was declared for June 27th, the day of Rathenau's State funeral. Throughout Germany, the universities closed, but in Heidelberg, Lenard's laboratory door stayed open. He declared: 'I cannot give my students a holiday just because of one dead Jew.' In Heidelberg, a small riot ensued. It was widely rumoured that Einstein was next on the assassin's list.

I wrote her a letter during the first days of our estrangement. I was in the Guest Quarters Suite Hotel on the Boston side of the Charles river, looking across to Cambridge and MIT and the brightening colours of the New-England fall. I had just come from Logan airport in a taxi and had taken a glass elevator twenty floors to my room. I told her in the letter that both the taxi and the elevator had carried me at the speed of light, but that no physical laws had been broken. Without her vertigo, her luggage, her whims, her moods, her threatened suicides, her temper, without all the leaden weight of our marriage, I weighed nothing, and felt free.

She sent me a proof copy of her latest short story. It came in the same post as her lawyer's first letter. The story concerns a vain, philandering hypochondriac:

> Every headache/meningitis
> Every backache/spinal cancer

An academic in his late thirties whose idea of a joke is to tell his young children that the Prime Minister of Ireland is called 'The T-shirt'. He constantly refers to these unfortunate children, in Cyril Connolly's phrase, as the 'enemies of his promise'. He proposes that, in a properly ordered world, sexual intercourse would be thirteen-a-side, like Rugby League. Twenty-six adults, working in shifts, might just entertain the average infant. In the story, after many such jokes, the man takes, and fails, a simple eye-test. That night, he dreams that the last unread line of the optician's chart contains the densely-encrypted story of the rest of his life. It is not a pleasant story, especially at the end:

> The prostrate gland/the surgeon's knife
> Whole saucepans of aluminium/embedded in
> his brain

and his children stay away from his graveside. She called the story 'John Donne's Glasses'. She scribbled on the title page that the boys both missed me and sent all their love.

You should not suppose that I am Einstein, the secular saint, and that she is Lenard, the paranoid fool.

You should not suppose that her father is Lenard's father, or that my science is Lenard's science. Our story is much more commonplace.

I suppose that every night millions of men and women lie awake sweating in their crisp clean sheets, bottled up on opposite sides of the bed like matter and anti-matter, afraid to touch, knee against thigh, hand against breast, for fear of their mutual annihilation in a soundless flash of gamma rays. I have lain many a night like that, listening to her sobbing in the warm perfumed darkness. I have prayed earnestly for my own death, encouraged its quick rush through my arteries to burst my miserable heart.

Now, we are parted. We shall never be severed.

In October nineteen thirty-three, Einstein sailed from Southampton for New York on the liner *Westernland*. Lenard's abuse pursued him across the Atlantic. Lenard wrote triumphantly in his *Deutsche Physik*: 'The Jew's theories are down and out. They were never intended to be true'.

Philipp Lenard had been a national socialist since nineteen twenty-four. He had written admiringly to Hitler when the Führer was languishing in prison after his abortive Munich putsch. Now, in matters of science, Hitler repaid the reverence:

> My Lenard, [he said] you alone of Men of Science have truly supported me from the beginning.

In the late nineteen thirties, on the eve of War, there were whispers that advances in physics, the children and grandchildren of the precious quantum, might make possible the construction of a new explosive device of quite terrible power which, if the Reich possessed it, would ensure forever its dominance of the world.

'My Führer,' laughed Lenard, 'this bomb is Jewish nonsense!' The same urgent rumours were abroad in America. In nineteen thirty-nine, besieged in his Long Island summer house by the frantic Leo Szilard, Albert Einstein reluctantly put his name to a warning to Roosevelt:

> Dear Mr President
> . . . A single bomb of the new type . . .
> . . . might destroy
> . . . a whole port and the surrounding country . . .

Lately, though the bottle empties, I find myself still dissatisfied. I pace the empty upstairs rooms. I talk to their dusty photographs, endlessly explaining and justifying things I hardly myself begin to understand. Mostly, my sentences begin: How could two such different people . . . ? and end up with shakes of my head.

Last question: what did we ever have in common?
Answer: two things.

First, we were both mammals. And second, and just as unremarkable . . .

Forgive your mother and father, my children. Einstein and Lenard made the modern world and, just as surely, our love made you.

THE HAMSTER

Linda McCann

Friday. The hamster is rolling about the grass in its clear plastic ball which, because of the air slots, would definitely not float in the goldfish pond. The cat watches from under a bush. A garland of birds is swinging between the telegraph poles.

It's getting cold now. I feel the cold through this cloth garden chair but whenever it's not actually pissing or frosty, people assume they have to sit outside and say what a lovely day it is and I, as always, am trying to appear normal. Well I'm away inside to be a warm headcase – they are on to me after all.

I dance to their tunes but I always seem to be the one left standing when the music stops – yes I'm here on my boyfriend's knee but his mother and sister let me know I'll never have my own seat. Oh, he thinks I'm being over-sensitive but this morning when I woke up, I opened my hand and the paper hankie was still there, seashelled into a lump.

In the pond, the frogspawn hangs like dusty bubble-wrap, breathing gently, rocking in the water clots, thicker than blood, and here and there a black comma curls tighter in its sleep.

My boyfriend's parents couldn't make it this weekend, so we're up here with just his sister – not the star status of the mother of course, but still a talented understudy.

And she's got the cat with her. They've even got a cat flap in the back door for when it's up here – a magnetic one, of course – only lets in the family cat.

That cat's certainly clever. Never bothers with the hamster, but then in the middle of the night it sneaks upstairs and leaves furry death threats – mouse and bird – along the wire bars at the top of the cage, each twisted neck, each tiny death expression saying 'You're next, hamster.'

Anyway, if his sister won the pools, she'd say 'Yeah. Just leave it there.' It's not just the family air of being unimpressed – for her it's an effort to associate with the other members of the world. The only reason I bother talking to her is that I don't want to appear to be intimidated into silence. She really is a big Balloon.

I mean, this morning, the two of us went to the shop. I do mean 'the' shop because the island only has one – one shop, one church, one one-track road (no pub). The shop closes at lunchtime on Fridays but still the Balloon had wasted the hours we had to spare and the long walk was making it look as if we'd never get there in time.

('In 562 A.D., Molouag and Columba arrived in the west coast of Scotland, looking for a suitable place from which they might spread the Gospel. Each realised the suitability of the island for this purpose and sought to be the first to land. When Molouag saw that his rival's coracle would reach the shores first, he cut off one of his fingers, threw it high onto the shingle and shouted "My flesh and blood have first possession of the island and I bless it in the name of the Lord." ')

The Balloon says that's a silly legend because if he'd cut off one of his fingers he'd have died of shock. Well I mean he'd have died of shock anyway when he saw there was no pub.

The sea was like diamonds, rolling on a strip of dark blue satin, then a trail of islands like stepping stones leading nowhere.

I mean it really is a lovely island and I said something about the flowers at the side of the road and she said what – the such and such? Did I not know they were such and such? And her silences added that I couldn't comment on them if I didn't know what they were called, as if pronouncing their name meant they belonged to her.

('A recent survey found over 293 varieties of wild flower on the island. St Molouag's flower, the Grass of Parnassus is still to be seen in late summer. More common flowers include: Tormentil, Scabious and Selfheal . . .')

And a similar seen-it-all-before-so-often-dear attitude on the way back, when we saw the baby lambs. I was standing at the fence, calling them to me, and I saw her tether-end disbelief, that militant vegetarian sneer that says I have a cheek to talk to lambs when I eat them – which I don't – right enough I've a cheek to talk to fish or chicken – but really, it's because she saw them as her lambs – as if her parents' having a holiday home meant they owned the whole island, a pay-off from investing years' worth of summers up there, instead of trying new places; intimate knowledge of the world's postage stamp without ever opening the parcel. They look down on daytrippers, while they grind into old ground until they feel they are in its soil – when really they've not scratched the surface of its doorstep.

When we reached the shop it was closing but the woman tried to sound cheerful when she said to me, 'Their mother's just the same.'

Didn't I know it. I bought a bottle of wine and was too embarrassed to buy anything else. But oh, the Balloon took her time – browsed – fingering postcards and reading ingredients, casually prodding the woman with questions, making her confess to a long list of items she didn't have in stock. They'd no fresh ginger? The Balloon smiled and crinkled her nose in coy disappointment. And the shop-keeper had to stand there patiently because this was a member of a family whose custom mattered, and that was what the Balloon was playing on, treating the woman as a servant, as trade.

It is a biblical landscape in pale washes of blue and grey. On the walk back from the shop, the pewter sky was held in a row of clenched white clouds, then the mist lifted and a white spine opened near the horizon, doubling the distance to the mainland. The land glowed and swelled, and far-off trees and hills breathed into existence, revealed as in the cleaning of the Sistine Chapel, or the pictures in a child's magic paintbook when swept with a wet brush. Battalions of pine strode the mountains in single file, browned at the edges, the turned pages of the centuries, and bookmarks of black water hung in ribbons that slowed to opaque silver.

('A little over a mile to the north of the church is Molouag's Chair. Tradition says that the saint often sat and meditated there. It is not hard to see why he chose this spot, for the view on a clear day is quite spectacular. "It will surprise you what the Lord has done." Sadly, the arms of this stone chair were broken off last century by a roadman looking for stone to mend the road.')

Saturday. Last night it was her turn to make the dinner, my turn to do the dishes. You should have seen all the pots, containers, bloody wooden spoons, making as much washing-up as possible, as if she'd run round all the nearest neighbours to borrow as many dishes as she could, as well as making it all look complicated as if she was Delia Smith – I mean who puts wee saucers of onions, mushrooms and herbs all over the place?

It reminded me of my Uncle Eddie. When he was a cook in the army, he had misread the ingredients for making rice – it was something like instead of ten cups, he put in ten sacks – and so when the mountains of cooked rice began to erupt, he billeted a group of soldiers to bury it. Later, when the sergeant major challenged the soldiers, 'Who called the cook a cunt?' one of them answered, 'Who called the cunt a cook?'

After dinner, the three of us were sitting in the living room, watching the hamster waltzing across the carpet. The Balloon hates it, is disgusted by the brown beads that collect inside the ball and roll among the dancing feet.

'And don't they produce a constant, invisible stream of urine?' she says – and yet it's only natural when her cat kills a whole nest of baby swallows, or last year when it took the blind eye out of an old farm dog – oh it must've attacked the cat first – oh sure: it never even had any teeth.

So, the hamster's rattling about the carpet – droning along the side of the bookcase – pinballing across to the skirting – keeping a high profile – 'Here I am cat – this is one furry sandwich you're not goany get.'

And the moggie's sitting in the middle of the floor ignoring him – washing the smudge on her face – and she gathers up her smoochiest sweetness – a smile quivering on her whiskers – a gala performance of chocolate-box perfection – and she's swooshing down, pulling herself round to reveal her white silk underside, gazing over to that luckiest owner in the world . . . and she's left angular and rigid upside down on the carpet and it's the hamster in a breathtaking Evel Knievel roll right over her soft fur stomach – onwards towards his audience, reaching and curtseying, waving his pink palms, radiant inside the spotlight of the moving ball.

Sunday. I'm sitting in the garden again, in the old cloth seat. Last night we were invited round for drinks by my boyfriend's ex-girlfriend, Fiona. The Balloon and Fiona, and my boyfriend and Fiona's brother, Fraser, had all grown up together, here, every summer, and Fiona and the Balloon had later studied at the same nursing college in Glasgow. Fiona just got married recently and she's up with her husband, her brother and her mum for a few days, staying at their country seat.

It was a damp cottage and the hallway was painted dark green. We were guided into a small living room which was a paler green and was half-filled by two fifties sofas, draped in faded sixties ethnic throws. A smoky fire struggled in the grate and a pot of soup sagged on a rusty electric cooker.

We all stood in the middle of the room as the introductions were made and the coats taken. I was being introduced to Fiona's brother Fraser, who was shaking my hand. His mother stood behind him.

The Balloon was leaning in front of me, smiling, almost jaunty. She was speaking to Fraser in Gaelic. I heard a word very similar to telephone and then several words later I heard her say my name.

'And do you not speak the Gaelic yourself Anna?' said Fraser.

'No,' the Balloon answered for me, 'she doesn't speak Gaelic.'

'The Gaelic,' I said and Fraser laughed.

'Don't you worry about it,' he said, 'for we'll all be speaking it soon when we're a nation again, eh?'

'Sit down Anna,' said the mother with a large and beautiful smile.

The Balloon continued to talk in Gaelic. Cheerful tones, smiles. Then she was introducing me to Fiona, smiling and waving her hand towards me, pausing now and then. But I understood the pauses. The silences were in the English.

There we were – all with Fiona in common – Fiona the perfect, best friend of my boyfriend's sister, sister of my boyfriend's best friend: in short, the one he should have married.

We sat down and were given a drink and for a long time the awkwardness was covered up by jokes and over-generous laughter.

I sat next to the brother's girlfriend. She was shy. I asked her if she'd met Fraser at university – yes – were they studying together – yes – then, a clever shift – what were they studying – but she just stated something like political philosophy and history, waiting for my next question, and then when I asked if she knew what she wanted to do and got my answer – no – I said it's a very good thing to study something because you want to, rather than to fulfil the requirements of some predetermined job – but still I got no real response for this, so I thought what am I dragging my bum leg around town for? These people see your effort as their tedious due, and they make you feel like an interrogator as they give you their hesitant smiles and sly looks, like someone shielding a head against blows, wishing you'd move on to someone else, so I did.

Then the mother was explaining that they didn't get up to the cottage as often as they'd like and they lived in a small town on the edge of Edinburgh.

Everyone else was talking about the rogue collie that had run away and was killing lambs. It was very unusual in being a lone killer, and also in being pure white, no markings, so that it had been nicknamed the White Devil. It was all pretty horrible. As well as the dead lambs, several sheep had to be destroyed as well; some had had their mouths torn off. The whole island was talking about it, like a city talking about the methods of the latest serial killer.

But Fraser was the real star of the evening. First of all, like someone giving a few pumping dry bokes before opening up and really spewing, he made some loud, ridiculously pompous declarations on various topics such as the Gulf War and the good aspects of the Poll Tax, all punctuated with advice such as we should read a history book, or didn't we read the papers, as if either told the truth.

Then he really got started. He had the loudest voice I'd
ever heard, talking over everyone in a monotonous super-
human drone. Like diced carrot in vomit familiar titbits
floated by, such as the Jews always take over and never
associate with non-Jews, or to call someone a nigger or a
paki is just the same as calling someone Jock or Taffy or
saying 'Oh, so you're from Aberdeen', and it was such a
solid wall of voice that it was difficult even to loosen a few
bricks.

His theories were well practised and he obviously found
them very dependable; like a cartoon character who has
complete confidence in his bike because he is as yet unaware
that he has cycled off the edge of a cliff.

'Paki,' 'Wog,' and 'Chinki' were not really racist words
at all, he concluded, if you don't intend them to be.

'I intended that pound note as a fiver, therefore give me
change of a fiver,' I said.

He said no, no, that people could determine the meaning
in this secret language system by looking at the context.

I said ' "I drove my table to work this morning" would
still incur the danger of someone taking you to mean a
wooden object with four legs.'

I was fascinated by his arrogance, his dogged stupidity
and his mounting rage that anyone could dare to contradict
him. He kept saying 'Come on! In educated company!'

His sister and mother seemed to sense an approaching
tantrum of some sort and they placated him in hushed
tones, casting me reproachful looks that said couldn't I see
I was upsetting him – he's not a naughty boy really if you
don't take his toys from him. They rephrased and sweet-
ened his precious words, telling him what he only meant,
but no, no, no, he would have the head off the gollywog,
and still the women looked at me, appealed to me as a
woman – sacrifice the gollywog to him then, what's one
little golly after all – it's only a load of wogs.

And meanwhile the mother was beginning to realize what
the debate was about. 'Yes,' she announced over everyone,

'we should be able to say "Paki".' Her voice was astonishingly loud and rasping and showed where her son got it from. She continued, 'And we should use it to mean exactly what it does mean – filthy, smelly, cheeky pigs who come over here and take all the business away from the white shopkeepers.'

Fiona put her head in her hands and then looked up to say, 'You see Mum doesn't know any coloured people and just because the Asian family at home who run the local shop just happen to be the only bad-tempered family in the town –'

My boyfriend interrupted: 'The only bad-tempered family? I bet old Mrs MacTavish up the road is very bad tempered. I bet the family three doors down can be a real pain in the neck.'

'No,' said the Balloon, 'I've been in that shop and they talk away in front of you in their own language – height of ignorance.'

'That's right,' shouted the mother, 'the family is a really really horrible family. They've had bricks put through their windows many a time.'

My boyfriend said, 'Yes, no one puts a brick through the nasty white families' windows – maybe it's their colour, not their nastiness?'

An uproar from Fraser the Oracle: 'It's got nothing whatsoever to do with colour.' He repeated this several times in the same blasting tones, in order not to lose the floor while he thought of what to say next, and I slipped in a calm 'Course it has' now and then to keep him going, make him spit and crackle like a faulty firework.

My boyfriend took this up, saying, 'It is to do with colour, with skin. I mean you get people who go into hospital and then they're horrified then they get a black doctor, black fingers examining them, touching them . . .'

Then it happened. I don't know if it was the word 'doctor', but at this point Fiona started listening carefully. There was a lot of noise in the room, voices trying to shout their way in, but she was nodding at my boyfriend as he continued, 'You get people who still think eeyeuch – black skin – it's as if it's covered in shite – it's alien, not human.' He rubbed his hands as if trying to get dirt off them.

'Yes,' she said, but, having completely misinterpreted his words and actions, she continued, 'I get quite – it gives me the shivers.' She held out her little hands and looked at them, palms and backs, and said 'When I work with black doctors, or treat black people – it's creepy, the black skin, you know?' She shuddered.

I was too shocked to answer so I just sat and looked at her.

'Oh but only if they're really black,' she said, 'only if they're really black.'

So it was just through embarrassment that she had cringed at her mother's words. The mother was giving the game away. Fiona had covered her face because her mother was a magnifying mirror in which Fiona caught sight of herself.

What bothered me most were the implications of what she had said, the assumptions about us that made her feel she could say it. In educated company. Her new husband remained silent.

('There are no rabbits, foxes or hares on the island. There are, however, many otters living around the shores. These are very shy animals and are not often seen. There is also a surprising number of buzzards.')

It's warm today. The sea is lapping and the island lies crouched in its humps of hills, flexing the segments of its tail of small islands like a sleepy dinosaur. The birds twitter in counterpoint, and flicker along the telegraph wires like notes on a page of sheet music, billowing across the blue. Each jagged flow of birdsong wobbles in the haze like an iridescent arch from a bubble wand. The hoody crows clump conspiratorially in a tree.

('A recent survey listed some 129 species of birds on the island. These include the Hooded Crow, Golden-Eye and Stonechat. Not all are present all the year round.')

In the pond the frogspawn is a city, its windows catching the light. I remember one night last summer when suddenly there were endless frogs, and then the next morning, scores lay squashed on the road, and we saw two that had been mating, flattened together into a star.

The pond is so clear today, dazzling on the surface and invisible underneath. The fish are asleep and the pebbles at the bottom are polished to reveal each speckle, each seam of rose and black. Water-lily clouds trail their shadows across the stone pondscape hills.

The hamster is still hamming it up, mincing around in its plastic ball. They got this one a ball when the cat killed the last one. Butcher of a cat. We'll all be sitting in the kitchen and then the cat flap will open and in it comes with a squeaking velvet vole – or a specimen of one of the 129 species of birds. My turn to make the dinner.

Monday. Our last day up here – the ferry doesn't run on a Sunday. A horrible thing happened yesterday. I feel awful sorry for her, the Balloon I mean. Susan's her name. She was standing at the kitchen window chopping her aubergines – God knows where she got them. We came running in when we heard her screaming, and when we looked out we saw the collie, pink eyes wild, white fur all red at the front like an elaborate ruby necklace, and something being shaken about in its jaws.

Then the White Devil was running away, and he flung up the dead body of the cat to thump behind him.

I heard a rolling noise. While my boyfriend was comforting his sister, I opened the kitchen door and looked at the cat flap. On either side of the opening was a strange scrape, a dent, as if something had been jammed there. Then I saw the red-speckled ball making for the fish pond.

AT THE TURN

Esther Woolfson

She goes out early. No-one will have heard her, not Jon, not Marie, not the dog who is old now, and becoming deaf. As she does, she knows immediately that it's a season at the turn. The sun's not yet out but when it is, it will melt away the strings of cloud looping the pine branches, alter the quartz-spangled rock into broken splinters of light under her feet. Soon, its heat will be gone. She recognizes, smells, a season ending. She's happy suddenly, realizing it's a chance seized at the last. She might learn, know, be free. A spray of fine dew flies from the mat grass and tormentils against her legs as she passes. The prospect of her clothes, still warm from her body, strewn across the rock, impels her on. The river under mist looks strangely alive, its insect haze hopping, seething over the water.

The place has the hum of death. She has always thought so. There's something not quite silent, something which makes her feel close to endings, not necessarily her own. She's grateful that at least the house is by the wide, open end of the glen, where there's definitely the hum but too faint to hear, where there's light and the beginning of the road to the town. It's deeper in, where you can go no further without climbing, which darkens, loudens, pitches her into feelings which she anticipates as she approaches. It hasn't just been since Rab told her his grim, invasive little tale. It's always been like that. She walks there reluctantly, even with other people, even on rare summer evenings when the light is golden and the hillsides spotted with tents and fires.

The place is so dark, most of the time, it's like the shutting of a giant eye. So dark there must be a micro-climate with different botanical laws. The darkness reveals the light so brilliantly that when it's bright, fireweed and hackberry and magnolia, foreign-sounding, probably southern plants she's read about in books, should spring from every place the light hits, even in the shadow of dense moss which coats the north sides of everything; stones, trees, walls, pours in soft green streams down roof slates, in between indented runnels of corrugated iron.

The light looks as though it should bring heat but rarely does. Usually, it's a wash of pure coldness. It hardly even has the power to melt, so, long after the town has cleared, there remain, often until well into what in other places is thought of as spring, banks of unrelenting snow, sly patches of camouflaged black ice.

On some warmer afternoons in winter, fingers of sun focus down thin beams of sodium brilliance, lighting up furred frost on black branches, ice-flaked leaves, fine wands of crystal grass. Then, it'll melt just enough for everything to begin to drip and the house is surrounded by an orchestra of dripping, from the rones and gutters, from the white-painted porch, the neat white side rails, along the line of glazing bars and lintels; trumming, tapping, ticking away the fabric of the day until the sun closes down and then, with a rapidity that is startling, shocking even, everything re-freezes. It goes silent, alters again into the motionless attitudes of petrification, glossy beads of water stilled in the act of dropping, condensation on a window engraved in ice, waterfalls suddenly solid, freeze-framed in the act of tumbling.

*　　*　　*

Occasionally, in past summers, she walked most of the way up the glen, a couple of miles or so, with Jon, her grandmother's husband and his meek, broken-spirited black-and-white dog.

Responding to Jon's yell, 'I go for a walk! Anyone to go with me?' her grandmother Marie always called up to her, 'Why don't you go with Jon dear?'

Her call always seemed to suggest it was both a pleasure which Marie, busy with cooking and chores, didn't have time to share and also that it would be a help if she did. Feeling that she couldn't refuse, she would come downstairs to see Jon stilled into silent, bubbling fury at Marie's reluctance and know he would say nothing to her on the walk. She knew, too, that he would lash his stick, one, two, three, within a single inch of the dog's backside, cursing in Ukrainian or Lithuanian or Latvian.

On those quiet evenings, she would ignore Jon and run up the narrow road, encouraging the dog to run beside her, slapping her leg, calling his name. He would follow, confident, almost skittish, till he remembered to stop, turning to look at Jon, jerked suddenly immobile on the end of his own, invisible leash of fear. Just like herself she thought once or twice, watching the dog. As soon as she had thought it, she suspected the thought, knew it to be both self-dramatizing and inaccurate. Her fears create no leashes, no limitations.

Where the hills converge at the head of the glen, they appear to her to close, to forbid, to warn you that you proceed with your life held precariously, in your own hands. The river seems to bear in its quick flow, threats, hints of power beyond reckoning. She's certain it's not hindsight. She broods on its mournful pools, its spates and torrents and knows that higher, for she has been up to them, there are brown, oily lochans, turbid ponds, subdued, marshy places whose darkness and unknown depth sink ineradicable channels in her thoughts.

She often wonders would she feel the same, would the burden be equal if she knew a bit less about each place, each rock, each stretch of river?

Rab has told her most of the odd things she knows about the area, things she wants to know as well as things she doesn't. Both their doctor and father of her closest friend, Elinor, his knowledge is legion and inescapable. His enthusiasm, certainly, is no less. The rampant eagerness and interest which appear to propel his life create a glow like a fire round him which he can't conceal, even by affecting his nonchalant, earnest kind of cool. She and Elinor laugh sometimes at his driven fascinations but follow him, nonetheless, up dull forestry tracks to obscure clearings, ancient sites of peculiar happenings, creep awkwardly behind him into dim, fungal caves from whose mildewed, odorous depth they can hear his distant voice, still talking. He tells them singular, recondite stories, of kidnappings and elopements, slayings and robbery, the enthronement of kings, of occasions when armies hid unseen and unheard or infants were abandoned and found again. After they've all been out together on Rab's free weekends, she has a new acuity, suddenly aware of time, of centuries heaping up, carelessly crushing down everything that has come before.

To tell them this particular story, he took them to a rock pool far up the glen where, three hundred years ago, a boy was drowned.

Mostly, Rob's stories flit and pass, leaving a meteor's trail of impression and memory, faint, starry and distant. Sometimes, she finds she can't remember enough of the detail to recount them the day after she's heard them. This one is different. It has become indelible and adhesive, and although she has plenty of other things she must think about, this one refuses to be displaced. It has taken root. It has begun to grow, to send a weedy, tangled presence winding through her brain.

One of the ways she recognizes its encroaching place in her mind is the way she thinks back, far too often, to the day Rab took them there. The day was a cool Saturday with high grey clouds drawing their shadows across the water, over the rock where he stood. She retraces the day from its beginning, reliving the moment of the story's telling. Rab transmitted the sense, she wasn't sure how, of having held it for a long time to himself, waiting for the moment of unburdening. He seemed gripped by analytic concern, fitting what he already knew to the details of place, discussing angles of the sun, times of the day, depth of water. He crouched on the rock, pointed, saying, 'Look, d'you see how the rock slopes down? He could well have gone in from here.'

After he told it, he seemed lighter, easier and it felt as if it were a burden he had handed on to her.

Lately, it has become easier for her to avoid the glen because Jon no longer walks. She takes the dog on her own, mostly into the town.

'Why not in the glen? A good walk for you both! Peace and quiet! Good air! The town? *Pzhja!*'

She has stopped saying she'll just walk him into town and instead omits to state a destination. She sets off up the glen, crossing to the road the back way, by Gibson's cottage. Often, she takes him to the shore and throws sticks into the clear water for him to chase. A saline crust forms along the fringes of his black fur and she combs his edges with a hairbrush as he dries. At other times, she walks him through the streets, stopping to talk to friends, watching constantly to see who might be watching her. The dog appears to enjoy being with her. She believes he is becoming more his own dog now that she has begun to encourage him in acts of rebellion. He won't ever turn on and rip his master to pieces, but will, with her at least, ignore a command or leap with wet legs against her front.

These days, she strolls along the fine stones of the beach. She doesn't run. She doesn't feel like it any more and knows that in any case, she couldn't ever run in quite the same way as she used to. It was different then, running up the glen road, a year, two years ago when she was still a child. Everything was open then, the sky, the road. It was before she began to feel that there must be someone watching her. In those days, you could be seen doing anything, running, with your hair dirty, wearing something awful, anything.

Also, it was before the arthritis which has proceeded to crumble all the joints of Jon's body. It has happened with terrible suddenness and she has learned not to think of the disease as a slow encroachment which creeps minutely along your fingers, round the sockets of your hips, decade by decade until you're old, bunched up like a pile of old tree roots and warty twigs. Jon's old, but she remembers keenly the strength he seemed to have until recently, a strength made unforgettable by the steely, pared-down threat of muscle under old skin. Swiftly, the disease has stolen the force of knuckle, ankle, wrist. He hasn't turned into a tree root. He's more like a big, jointed doll whose axis is bending, beginning a tilt which, in time, will prove fatal. From the look of him, the disease seems to be working methodically, neck, spine, hips and elbows.

Rab says that no-one knows what causes it and that the person who discovers will win the Nobel prize. She wonders if she might give winning it a try one day. There are times when she is tormented by anxiety in case someone else will find out and win it before she has a chance. With a view to this, she keeps an eye on Jon, fixing on his stoops and angles, noting the constant mutations of geometry. Nowadays, he has a looseness about him which makes him seem as if his wires are developing sags and fraying, his bolts losing their ability to hold. She thinks she can hear the easy clack of bone on bone, the slow, mitigated grind of muscle over cartilage. He does everything with difficulty; walking, sitting, bending. He is to have his hips renewed in Glasgow, but secretly she has diagnosed that hips won't be enough and soon he'll need it all.

Often, she ponders on the possible causes. Marriage is one though it seems more of a coincidence. Her grandmother's food? Perhaps his joints liked, thrived on stew and gluey bread. Perhaps Marie's miraculous food has overloaded a naturally austere system. She knows nothing of his heredity. His genes are mysterious and isolate. Her own, on the other hand, are predictable and she observes, even now, the line map of the way she will come to look forming on her mother's face, as it already has on Marie's.

They have been married for five years, Jon and Marie. Her first life ended with their marriage. It's strange to her because everything she remembers about that life makes her feel as if it was lived by someone else. The packing of her old room in the flat she shared with her mother and Marie into a neat series of boxes brought about the folding, the closing down of her first life. Her second, different life is here, in this room in Jon's house, in a room he equipped and decorated specially for her. Her mother is in another small flat, in Glasgow this time.

Rab comes in from time to time to check on Jon's progress. His broad body always appears to be attempting to escape from the formal clothes he wears to work. Tucking his shirt back into the waistband of his suit trousers, he bends to look at Jon who is instantly mild and grateful, quelled by

79

the irreducible power of knowledge. Meekly, he yields up his failing joints for Rab's examination.

'Any pain in your hands? Any weakness?'

The afternoon Rab took them to the pool was intermittently bright with high clouds turning to dark blue-grey. Later in the afternoon, when they were home, it began to rain, one of the blistering, penitential downpours of early summer. While Rab was telling his story, Elinor hovered a distance away, pottering in the ditch, freer, with less need to be politely attentive. Eventually, she stood up and waved, displaying a small black object discovered in the grass.

'Nobody very exciting, just one of the weevil family,' she called over, displaying the quivering dot on her hand. She bent to put it back.

On the way home, Rab repeated the story for her, details, contemporaneous descriptions:

'His face towards the rays of the sun,' 'as if he were asleep.'

'Oh God, spooky,' Elinor said.

She watches Rab examine Jon, notes the pressure of fingers, the sequence of questioning. It has been a while since she began wondering about Jon. She regards it as one of the penalties of adult consciousness which she knows is upon her and now, will never go away. It has made her suspicious and unaccepting, aware of soughs and mires filling and draining in constant dreadfulness beneath the surface of virtually everything.

She remembers Jon first from the sawmill. This is so long ago, she recalls with surprise, that there is no part of her memory which pre-dates Jon. Unreal then, it was a place which may never have existed, all noise and strangeness and dangerous magic. They went, she and her mother and Marie, on Saturday afternoons to buy logs for the fire. She remembers it from the earliest flash of memory, dark-interiored, musty barns, whining, murderous machinery, pale, shifting pyramids of sawdust, then a tall, light-eyed presence loading logs into the high boot of the car, the presence in time becoming Jon, Jon who disappeared into the low wooden house to bring out packets of sweets for her, Jon talking to her mother and Marie, Jon bending, smiling, closing the car doors securely, standing back, waving after them on the road.

Weird people worked there, everyone said, birds of passage, odd-bods, DPs.

Older people who had lived through the war talked about displaced persons. Their voices seemed to her to contain faint irritation, fainter sadness.

Her mother and Marie would clutch her up and hold her to let her see through the windows of the sawmill workers' house, to a crepuscular scene of dim light, a child's storybook illustration of wood stove and long refectory table set with plates and cutlery and the packets of bread she now thinks may, after all, have ruined Jon.

They used to stand to watch the machines split and slice and slew out dust and planks and neat-cut logs. 'You must have a care here!' Jon always yelled above the screech and groan. 'I see a man once, huh, sckrrrrrrr! Like that log,' indicating against his own broad body, graphically, a horrible dividing, a slitting, head to toe.

Later, she began to see Jon about the town working in other places, at the boat-hire in summer, driving the fish lorries, behind the counter of the shop which in time became his and from which he earned the money which has allowed him to buy the house, marry, live as they do now.

* * *

Marie does everything for Jon without appearing to. It's a skill she must have learned through prolonged contact with husbands and pupils and querulous children, the art of concealing almost constant activity, making it seem without effort. It's her second marriage, so she's had some practice. It's Jon's first and perhaps because it has happened so late, he appears, in spite of himself, to be trying hard. Marie is kind though, a conciliator. She says that she's always been quiescent, gone along with people for the sake of peace. She says she recognizes it in herself but feels nonetheless that if more people were like her, there would be fewer wars. Marie remembers the last one, just, and says she would kill herself immediately if another war like it began.

'How would you do it?'

'Honestly, the things you ask!' Marie says, but never answers.

She suspects that Marie doesn't know. She could suggest a few ways, a few things to take, but doesn't.

The boy who drowned was about sixteen. He was small by accounts of the day, Rab said, fair-haired and of particular beauty. This is mentioned in all the references Rab has discovered. He was missing for a month before he was found.

Since Jon's illness, she has taken it upon herself to do the work in the garden which Jon can no longer do. She's not sure why but she thinks it's out of goodness and decency.

Regularly, she offers to carry out the more arduous tasks, the pruning, the necessary double digging of early spring, hefting his heavy spade, the warm wooden handle of his garden fork moulding now, she feels, to the shape of her own hand. Marie, who doesn't have time for gardening, whispers, 'Don't you do it. I'll get a man in,' but she wants to do it. The idea of masochism interests her.

* * *

Like an ancient forge-master, Jon stands imperiously over her, pointing with his stick, 'There, now there, this bit not done enough,' as she digs. She makes a fine job of it, chopping through the pliant earth, carrying spadefuls of malodorous, rotted goo at a run across the grass but afterwards, as he mutters to Marie, she wonders if he is complaining. It's the way he talks, odd, sibilant, Baltic sounds, *tszk!* and *hcszha!* and *chrshtse!* When she's impatient with him and stops for a moment to lean on her spade, she often takes the time to stretch, her whole body muscling upwards under her jeans and T-shirt, arms lifting to the sky. Her wiring is fine and taut, her bolts tight as wheel-nuts.

Sometimes, she watches Jon walking about in his garden. His walk makes her think of the words 'terrible pain'. His joints have rooted him, formed an invisible cage around him. She feels his frustration rise in a cloud from him as she watches, usually from the window in the upstairs hall which has two square panes of red-stained glass set into the top. The sun shining through the glass makes falls of watery blood drip and waver down the grey carpet of the stairs. Sometimes she just stands for a moment looking down, seeing Jon very small, insignificant against the infinite marvel of his creation.

Often, she wonders about Jon.

Since she has come to live here, she wakens early at weekends to make breakfast for Marie and Jon. She gazes out at the walkers passing by the house. Their clothes, their boots, are expensive things, their colours, purples and turquoises and yellows, brilliant exotica against the darkness of tree and stone.

Jon despises climbers, hates climbing. He says he can see no point in it. Nowadays, he's careful not to say it in front of Rab who is an experienced, accomplished climber. In the days when he still gardened vigorously, Jon used to stand scowling by the front fence on weekend evenings in spring and summer to protect his plants against the climbers who he said plundered his bushes for cuttings.

Washing up after Sunday night supper on winter evenings, she watches headlights, low beams of crossing light which glare briefly across the window. The drone of rescue vehicles grows, passes, then recedes.

'Another come to grief!' she'll hear Jon say. The way he says 'grief' sounds to her like 'Crieff'. When she heard it first, she began to laugh and told Elinor at school the next day.

'The Jon vision of the afterlife, *El Paradiso*.'

For years, when she was little, she and her mother would go by bus to Crieff for Christmas shopping and tea in an hotel. 'Nearer than Glasgow,' her mother used to say, but now, distance diminished, they wander round Glasgow instead and go back to her mother's tiny flat where she sleeps the two or three nights on the uncomfortable sofa-bed.

Jon thrills to the climbing deaths. 'Oh, dreadful, dreadful,' he will be saying all morning round the town, in the shops and the bank, 'I hear it, so much noise in the night.'

She knows he will have heard nothing. His and Marie's room is at the back and anyway, his growing deafness has stopped him being aware of distant, or even approaching, sound.

She has listened though. Engines running, water, the sound of breathing. She wakens before light, cold as a stone, pinned tight by apprehension.

*   *   *

She has begun to think about water What it is and does.
Specific gravity, depth, movement, unyielding weight.

He was found, Rab said, on the first sunny day after rain.
The sun slanting into the water illuminated the white face;
the white body half-emerged onto the surface of the full,
swelled pool.

Knowing this makes the place mutate, creates a spark, an
electric charge between curiosity and longing. This boy,
pale in the sunlight. She tells herself she won't think about
it but does anyway.

Now, when she's reading, she becomes maddeningly aware
of her own breathing. She stops, draws in breath, holds,
waits. She knows it's only a small way to knowing. This,
in deep water, in darkness, everything failing, falling, everything giving way. Even before she needs to, she draws in
breath, hearing the sound of her heart loudening in her
ears.

Three hundred years since the drowning. Twenty-one times
the span of her life. Plus a few decimal points.

She asks where he's buried but Rab doesn't know.

The trees are distant enough from the garden to form a
background, far enough not to cast permanent shadow. A
deep cleft in the mountains allows the sun to reach, makes
Jon's flowers, his grass, his cabbages grow.

She remembers that when she was small there were a
few people still talked about as 'DPs'. She doesn't know
where the others are now and doesn't ask. The words
themselves, Displaced Person, seemed a summation of
loss and hopelessness and made her think of discarded
toys mislaid by indifferent children. For Jon, this has

ceased to be and not only is he not displaced, he seems to her to be seigneurial, imperial over soil, wall and roof tile.

He does, though, still seem to her to be oddly solitary. Towards that, she has a sense of understanding. She wonders if he has relatives still alive, if he appears, even now, in some enduring, indestructible store of familial memory.

For a while after she came to live in his house, she watched the post daily for the kind of mean-looking envelopes people might use if they didn't have much to write on, strange stamps, foreign postmarks, telling addresses. There must have been a family once, however ragged and unsatisfactory, but they give no sign of themselves. There are no indications, as far as she can discern, that any effort has been made to find Jon, and it has been fifty years.

Not long after Jon and Marie's marriage, the Demjanjuk trial began. She remembers it now as part of the foundation bed of memory of her new life. She saw it on the news on the large colour television Jon had proudly bought for his bride. She began to think about it then, waiting every day to see if it was mentioned on the evening news. Watching, she pondered the unknowability of people.

She observed Jon watching the trial, the news since about Demjanjuk. It has always appeared to be the same as his watching the news about everything; 'Why they tell us this, heh? Who interested?'

She thinks very often of the figure in the open-necked shirt sitting, sweating and bewildered in the dock.
'I wonder if he really was Ivan the Terrible,' Marie always says.

'Eh, who know?' Jon replies confidently. 'Cunning bas-
tars, these people.'

There were news reports, documentaries, film footage. She
watched and thought for a long time about what she saw.

Three hundred years. She counts graph-paper squares in
endless variations, each square a year between her life and
his. Together, they look a small collection, too brief, too
short for obliteration or forgetting.

His body was naked when they found it. That was the
shame, Rab told her, shaking his big head at the strangeness of it. The shame of his nakedness. They had tried to
say his clothes had come off in the water, moved gently to
and fro by the falling of the spring from the rock but later,
they found his clothes, whatever they wore then, trousers
and boots and shirt, whatever, strewn along the hillside. It
took Rab a few minutes to tell the story, his big body
crouching over the edge of the dark pool, but it has taken
him years of reading and searching and piecing together
bits of books and manuscripts and church records to try to
understand this ancient incident. His way of telling it was
detailed but with areas of vagueness. Inexplicably, she felt
as though she had lost someone, a grief spanning three
hundred years. As he told it, she felt waves of a cool fear
pass down and down her body.
  'He was found in the early morning. The sun would have
struck here, if you think that it rises, east, over there.' She
stood and looked down, the light falling in bars of dusty
brilliance through the water's still surface.

Throughout the rain of that evening, she saw his body
glowing, pale, nacreous under green water.

She thinks of what there is to separate them. Nothing more
than centuries, nothing more than time. She is constantly

aware of walking the same contours of river and hill, seeing the same bleak outlines of a landscape changed less by age than other places.

It was modesty which made them want to believe that water could take clothes off a body, Rab said. Sleeve by sleeve, button perhaps by button, if they had buttons, ties and cuffs and waistbands, she isn't sure, this way and that, edging fabric from skin. They must have known that it couldn't, not water on its own. Sea perhaps, with its violence and currents, but not that water whose danger lies in its stillness and its depth.

They were well to do, the family of the drowned boy. Rab has told her that that's why he knows of them, that the rich are easier to trace back, that they leave records, evidence of their lives, solidly, in stone and paper. It's the poor she thinks of mostly, traceless people who have left not a stir on the earth's surface. And then this boy, living in her mind after three hundred years.

'Sounds nice, don't you think?' Elinor says. 'Fancy drowning. What a waste.'

There are certain evenings when she understands the pure, wild joy anyone could feel on a spring evening, a warm spring evening when, after winter, everything is new and possible. The climate would have been better then, Rab has said. You could easily fling off the restraint of garments and a closed, tight church Sunday and run and run, your feet probably hardened already to twigs and stones, skimming, flying over areas of grass and heather; springy, damp bog sending your footsteps on. The water would rise brown, seeping against the portion of your toes which, just for a moment, touched down. No bits of glass, no rusting Coke cans, knots of barbed wire, blown fertilizer sacks. She can imagine what she would feel like, if there was no-one, no-one possibly in the world to see her, after a nuclear explosion or the plague, when she was definitely the only person left and she could run and run as he might have done, along the line of the hill, fit and pale and beautiful as she is and she wonders what a boy feels like, running. She has always wondered.

If that's what it was, joy, wildness, an angry, exuberant rush towards freedom, something urgent, purposeful. If he took his own clothes off, climbed into the water, tried to swim. There are other possibilities.

She thinks of the way the air stops, the light. An endless stream of drowning.

She has been back since Rab told her the story. Once or twice. Just to look.

'Mmm,' Rab says, the bones of Jon's wrist held between his fingers, 'can you feel this? And this?' She pays attention to his voice which manages cheer but hides something, hopelessness perhaps, or despair.

She has never known how Jon came to be here. When she asked her mother or Marie, as soon as she realized that the way he spoke was foreign not simply eccentric, they were hesitant and unsure and made her wonder if they knew. They talked about great movements of population, forced labour, invasion and destruction. They told her how people lost places which had been theirs. She was fascinated and horrified but ended up not knowing why it was that Jon was here and why, once the war was over, he hadn't gone back.

Jon and Marie's marriage has changed her life, her mother's life.
    'She can come to us,' Marie had said. 'Jon's very fond of her. A new start for you.'
    Her father, who she doesn't know, is somewhere he

doesn't write from, in Brunei perhaps, or Qatar, or rebuilding Kuwait.

She goes to the library quite often when she's in the town, riffling through the shelves, sitting in the murmuring quiet, the dog tied up outside, lying easefully across the warm, grey pavement slabs. Her taste is eclectic but whatever she reads while she's there, she leaves feeling both canny and ignorant at the same time.

Since his marriage, she has asked Jon a few times about his life. When Marie isn't there.
'Don't ask,' Marie has warned her, not just once.

She waits for Christmas and Easter. These, she believes, are the seasons of reminiscence and returning, when she thinks he might be tempted into a net of memory. Each time, she plans to beguile him into nostalgia for his childhood, to remind him, tempt him to recall. There must be things – the consolation of family, the rites of a church which long ago was his, with all the forgotten, clutching ardour of guilt and forgiveness. She always frames her questions carefully so that they appear artless and casual.
'Heh!' is all he has ever said, looking at her with his pale eyes. 'Gone all that. No good.'

She bears everything in mind, observing Jon across the dinner table. He insists on a formality which she realizes he has learned, as if he's watched for a long time what other people do. Theirs is a household with butter knives, crystal glasses and engraved silver napkin rings at every meal. These items are all stored in the boxes in which they were recently bought, or given as wedding presents. She knows that her grandmother never lived like this in the more chaotic days of her early childhood and so their lives have the distant feeling of playing house.

*   *   *

She recasts him from time to time. Admits possibilities.

'We'll have to do something about this, Jon,' Rab says, gently moving Jon's numbing foot.

There are clips sometimes of disputed identity cards, photos showing Demjanjuk as a very young man. Jon would have been very young then. Bright-eyed, broad-faced.

She repeats formulae to soothe herself. That if it were true, she'd be able to tell. She'd know. Surely. That whatever he's done, he isn't going to do again with his crumbling wrist joints and wobbling head.

In summer, Marie and Jon sit together on stout wooden chairs on the grass, which she cuts and edges late in the evening while it's still light. Pipistrelles criss-cross the garden, tiny, flying flickers of night. There's a good lawn-mower and electric edger and so the lawn looks wonderful. Even now, Jon follows, limping, a step behind her, pointing out a bit which could do with more attention, smoking a cigar to keep away the midges, its lit end bright in the growing darkness.

'See? No damn flies! A good service I provide? No?' and the cigar, a dash of fire, curves a circumscribed line through the night air.

Companionship is what Marie said she was marrying for, when she first told her. She still thinks about it, though she doesn't yet know the component parts of companionship. Of loneliness, she has some ideas.

They said his face looked as if he were asleep. After a month in the water, she knows, he wouldn't look asleep.

Staying overnight at Elinor's, she creeps occasionally towards Rab's overflowing study at what must be two, three in the morning. Before the birds. She sits awhile among the heaps of books and papers, foraging. Sometimes Jill, Elinor's mother hears and comes out of her room, frousled and concerned. 'What is it angel, are you all right?'

She says yes, fine, she can't sleep or she's on her way to pee, suddenly conscious of the way her life is bounded in with questions and care and by daunting vigilance. Her mother will be in her small flat in Glasgow, possibly alone.

It is in a newspaper that she reads idly one afternoon in the library, an article about the prosecution of war criminals. She chills and promises herself that she will not brood. Many, it says, entered the country as displaced persons. From the Baltic, the Ukraine. Some had their blood group tattooed under their arms, the ineradicable, for many have tried, mark of membership of the Waffen SS.

'For companionship,' Marie still tells her, pleadingly almost, 'I just didn't want to be on my own forever. You'll be away soon.' Marie is fit and quite young and to her eyes, still pretty. The doors are stout, wooden and firmly closed at night and she sleeps at the other end of a long corridor.

She realizes that she will never know. The letters of a blood group, tattooed under the left arm. She tries to recall swimming, to the days when Jon worked brown and shirtless on summer afternoons, but nothing has fixed itself to her memory and she berates herself for her lack of attention to detail. Any mark would now be concealed by the soft folds of skin which have resulted from the drastic implosion of Jon's bones. She thinks fleetingly of asking Rab but knows what he will say. Gravely, I'm sorry, I can't.

She has never seen Jon's passport. She doesn't know if he has one or what it is.

*   *   *

In Edinburgh on a school trip to the theatre, she spends her half an hour of free time in the medical bookshop among pages of orthopaedics, rheumatology, neurosurgery. Afterwards, on the bus north, the X-rays stay in her mind, grey shadows turning to skull and spine, white bone flowering from darkness. Names repeat themselves again and again, bone cutters, laminae, granulation.

There have been moments when she has wanted to ask, to say; almost beginning a sentence, stopping, as if her words were icicles which had begun to melt in unusual warmth but then, like twigs, flowers, water, had begun re-freezing. She will spoil something and so she keeps these particular thoughts warm and liquid and moving around in her mind, never letting them spill to wreak caustic, disfiguring damage.

She has gone there, looked into the still pool, once or twice. No more than centuries, nothing more than time.

'Don't ask,' Marie says, as if she knows.

She awakens in the night and hears rain teeming into water, twigs cracking under an unknown weight. Conscious of the rhythm of her breathing, she stops, counts and falls asleep.

Marie will look after Jon, watch him as his legs fail and his arms. They will replace his hips and then fuse and wire and set his neck, once, and it will fail as his joints come apart, twice and then there will be insufficient bone to wire, and then no more and she will be alone.

Sitting up in bed, wide-eyed in opaque darkness, she knows. It's not only time that separates them, not only an arc widening, growing slowly, daily more between them. They are separated by knowledge, experience.

*　　*　　*

It's early when she goes out. No-one stirs, not even the dog who is elderly and, like Jon, is becoming deaf.

There has been rain lately, the brief warm rain of summer ending. The river's insect haze shimmers. Clouds of midges and water boatmen streak the glass surface. The low finger of unmoving cloud is beginning to disappear now, the loops of mist draped over rock faces melting in the early sun.

Her rucksack, thudding on her back, makes her feel foolish and self-conscious though she sees nobody. After short reflection, she abjures the run along the hillside. There are rusting Coke cans and skeins of wire and as yet, no mushroom cloud has removed the possibility of watchers.

It's nothing, taking her clothes off on a rock. She does it every summer, swimsuited, beside another, brighter pool. It is an effort, just at first, not to fold her clothes. Flinging becomes easier as she does it, garment by garment. Being naked, standing up naked is different and she turns her body to the light and smiles and slowly holds her arms up, laughs and says to herself, I must be mad, remembering again why she's here, lowering herself onto the rough, quartz-grained rock, her toes curling, gaining hold, standing back from an overhang of grass which could tumble her into the water. In any case, she can swim. She smiles again. She sits down and lowers her feet into the water, soft brown round the crumbling bank, water plants rotted into sludge clouding round her ankles, melting particles of floating vegetable dust.

The place still hums with a vibration she recognizes but it's beautiful from here, still dark this early, even though the sky is lightening.

Warmer than she imagined, the water draws her easily in. Her feet fade into the brownish, greenish aqueous distance, one arm lying white along its dark surface. Opening her eyes wide, she releases her hand-hold on the rock.

She knows suddenly that it's not from affinity that she's here, holding her arms straight up, sinking, it's from something else entirely.

Under the green water, light floats down towards her, in snatches. She wonders for a moment if he was alive when he entered the water. If he wasn't, he has moved beyond her imagination, out somewhere she can never know. Three hundred years, the rock only so eroded, water evaporating, filling in endless formation of season and year. Under her feet, there is nothing but water, her arms submerged, the brown light dimming.

Waiting for her on the grass in her rucksack is the rug from the end of her bed, a bath towel, her hairbrush, a tin of talc.

Waiting for her is everything she can think of, the Nobel prize, destiny, some strange inheritance she's bound to make for herself.

Looking up, she sees the world as through a fish's eye, a lens of translucent brightness, a net of light and water. As he must have seen it, if he drowned. His last glance on earth. She still hasn't touched the bottom but her breath is going. She surfaces quickly, shooting up into the light and swims easily to the place where Rab says his body was found. Turning, she lies there, her back against the rock. The spring, started up again by the summer rain, runs a stream of ice over her head and down between her shoulders. Like a child, she begins kicking both feet, raising rainstorms of sparkles, glassy, spangly drops which cascade from her toes, liquid timpani as they fall back into the pool. She lifts her chin and closes her eyes, absorbing in through her eyelids and forehead, the last of the season's sunlight.

FAT DATE

Alexander McCall Smith

He stood before the door, peering at the small brass plate above the bell. It was undoubtedly the right place, but he had expected something more than this somewhat anonymous sign. Still, that was an indication of good taste and discretion, which was exactly what one wanted from such a concern. It was a question of tact, really; the last thing one would want of people like this was flashiness or vulgarity.

He rang the bell and waited, examining a small notice that somebody had pasted to the wall: STAIR CLEANING. IF IT IS YOUR TURN, PLEASE REMEMBER TO MAKE SURE THAT YOU . . .

'Mr Macdonald?'

'Yes.'

She smiled at him, not too enthusiastically, but just enough to set him at his ease.

'Do come in. We were expecting you.'

He followed her along a small corridor to an office which overlooked the square. It was full summer, and there were trees outside the window, a shifting curtain of deep green. He took in the surroundings immediately. An office, but a *personal* office. There was a vase on the top of the filing cabinet, filled with a spray of carnations. Carnations: exactly right. You might have expected roses in a place like this, but that would have been too obvious.

'Please sit down.'

She was behind her desk now, and she had opened a file in front of her. 'You haven't said very much about yourself on your form,' she said.

He glanced at the piece of paper in her hand, recognizing his rather spidery writing. 'I feel a little bit embarrassed writing about myself,' he said. 'You know how it is.'

She nodded, gesturing with her right hand as if to say: of course we understand; everybody here is in the same boat.

'You see,' she said, 'we like to get things just right. It's really no good introducing people if they have radically different views of the world. Even a slight difference in musical taste may have a dramatic effect on the way in which people get on.'

'Jack Spratt and his wife,' he said, and then stopped. The words had come out without his thinking, but he realized immediately that the reference was ill-chosen. Jack Spratt could eat no *fat*, and his wife could eat no lean.

But she did not notice. 'Yet in our case,' she went on, 'we have a good starting point. By catering specially for larger people, we manage to get round what some people see as a difficulty. If people have the same general *conformation*, then they start off with at least one thing in common.'

He nodded. Yes. That was why he had chosen them. Perhaps he should not mince his words, at least when thinking. This was an agency for fat people. Dating for fatties! There, he had thought it! What would she have said if he had dared to say it? She would have written him off, no doubt, as a person with an attitude difficulty or a self-image problem.

'Now, I do have a few possible introductions for you,' she went on, looking at him over her half-moon glasses. 'There is one lady, in particular, an extremely charming person. I know her well. She and you share an interest in opera, I believe. She was married, some years ago, but sadly she is now divorced. It was really not her fault at all.'

'It never is,' he said. 'It never is the stout person's fault.'

A frown crossed her brow quickly, but then she smiled.

'There are awful injustices committed against more generously proportioned people,' she agreed. 'It was certainly so in this case.'

They talked for a few more minutes. She served him coffee, poured from a tall white coffee percolator, and offered him a delicate chocolate biscuit. He took two and immediately apologized. 'I seem to have picked up two,' he said.

She waved her hand. 'Please. Think nothing of it. I have a weakness for chocolate too. Our shared little vice.'

Now he stood outside the theatre, glancing nervously at his watch. She had said on the telephone that she might be a little late, but he had not expected to wait for fifteen minutes. If they were not careful, they would miss the beginning of the opera, and would not be admitted until the first interval. The possibility worried him. How would he entertain her in those awkward first few minutes. At least going to the opera gave them something to do.

But she had arrived now, leaping lithely out of a taxi in a shimmer of light blue voile.

'Edgar?'

He reached out and shook her hand.

'Nina?'

She held his hand for a few seconds longer than was necessary. 'I knew it was you,' she said, adding: 'I'm so sorry for being late.'

He thought for a moment. How did she know it was him? There could have been other men waiting – the street was by no means empty – but then he realized what it was. He was the only person in front of the theatre who could possibly have come from the introduction agency for fat people. He found the simple explanation unutterably depressing.

They went into the theatre. There was the usual opera crowd, some of whom he knew. He found this reassuring, and helpful. She noticed that people nodded to him and waved. I'm not a nobody, he thought. People know me about town.

'There's Fatty Macdonald,' whispered one man to his wife. 'Nice chap. Bit of an uphill battle, though.'

'How do you know him?' the wife whispered back.

'Work?'

'No, school. He was a year above me. We used to call him names and torment him too – you know how boys are. He had a terrible time, poor chap. Perhaps we could have him round for dinner some day and make up for it.'

'I can't, I just can't. I've got *so much* to do. Look at next week, for example . . .'

They found no difficulty in making conversation during the interval. He was pleased to find that there was no awkwardness, as one might well expect on an occasion such as this. It all seemed wonderfully natural.

'I must confess I felt some trepidation,' she said. 'I've only had one or two introductions through them before. I'm not used to it.'

He looked at her. 'I've never been before. Ever.'

'Well, you must have been feeling very nervous.' She dug him playfully in the ribs. 'Go on, confess!'

He laughed. 'Well, I suppose I did. You never know how things are going to work out.'

'Well, there you are,' she said. 'It really isn't awkward at all.'

After the final curtain, they left by the side exit and walked briskly down the street to the Italian restaurant where he had booked a table. He explained to her that the place had been recommended by friends and that they specialized in after-theatre suppers.

'What a treat!' she said. 'A wonderful way to spend a Tuesday evening!'

'Monday,' he corrected.

They both laughed.

'Well, Tuesday as well, if you'd like...' He stopped. No. It was far too early to invite her out again. There should be a cooling-off period of a few days before he telephoned her and issued an invitation. That was what he had been told at the agency. 'Don't rush matters,' he had been warned. 'You've plenty of time to think things over. And women don't like being rushed either. Just wait until you've both had a certain amount of time to think about how you feel about one another.'

In the restaurant, the proprietor led them to their table and drew her seat back with a flourish. She ordered a glass of sherry and he asked for a gin and tonic. Then they sat and looked at one another.

'I love Italy,' she said. 'I can't wait to go back there again. Florence. Siena. Verona.'

'Rome,' he said. 'Venice. Bologna.'

'Ah. Perugia. Urbino.'

They were silent for a moment, while they both thought of something to say.

'I rented a house there once,' he said. 'I took it for two months and did nothing but sit on the terrace and read. I read and read.'

'Ah.'

'And then in the evenings I'd walk down to the piazza and watch everybody else watching everybody else.'

'They're quite amazing,' she said. 'The Italians. They *amaze* me. They literally *amaze* me.'

The silence returned.

'Do you like Italian food?' he asked. 'I do.'

'Oh, I do too,' she said. 'The herbs!'

'And olive oil,' he added. 'There is no substitute for olive oil, there really isn't.'

'Edgar, I quite agree with you. There really is no getting round it. You have to use real olive oil. You simply have to.'

* * *

They ate well. She laughed as he struggled with his pasta; she had no trouble with it on her own fork.

'I just can't do this,' he said. 'I'm hopeless.'

'I'll teach you one day,' she said. 'It *is* a bit of an art.'

They raised their glasses to one another and sipped at the chilled Orvieto, sharp, straw-coloured. He imagined that he saw the colour of the wine go straight into her eyes, and she liked the idea.

'Perhaps it does,' she said. 'Anyway, what a nice thought!'

They drank more wine, and the proprietor brought a fresh bottle, tucked into its damp envelope of ice. Then, over coffee, he said: 'I must say that I was quite relieved to discover the agency. It really isn't easy if you're on the larger side. People seem not to want to know.'

She nodded: 'It's so unfair.'

He warmed to his theme. 'You know, thin people sometimes don't realize how cruel they're being. They laugh at us. They call us names.'

'Yes,' she said. 'When I hear a child calling somebody *Fatty*, I say to him: "Just you think how you'd like to be called that! Just you think!" But most of the time they just can't imagine how other people feel.'

He reached for the rest of the bottle of wine and filled their glasses.

'I was called names at school,' he said.

'How awful,' she said. 'What were they?'

He glanced away. 'I forget now,' he said. 'It was a long time ago. But if you think about it, you can't really blame children. They just take their cue from adults. Adults had it instilled in them when they were children, and so the vicious circle is perpetuated.'

'And books contribute to the problem,' she said. 'Look at the way stout people are portrayed in fiction.'

He nodded enthusiastically. 'They describe us in an uncomplimentary way. They use words like *waddle* when they want to describe how a stout person walks. And films too. Look at the ridiculous things that happen to stout people in films. Absurd, slapstick things – people falling over, getting stuck and so on. As if life were like that!'

'You must have had an awful time,' she said. 'Imagine being called names at school.'

He felt puzzled and rather annoyed by her referring to his childhood. And he thought that she shouldn't have asked him what his nickname was. That was really rather intrusive.

'Why do you say *I* must have had a difficult time,' he said, rather peevishly. 'You must have had a tough time too.'

'Me?' Her eyes opened wide with surprise.

'Yes. After all, you're just as stout as I am.'

Her jaw dropped. 'I beg your pardon,' she said, her voice suddenly icy. 'I certainly am not.'

He put down his glass and stared at her, astonished. 'Oh yes you are. If you ask me, you're possibly even fatter.'

'Oh! Oh!' She lifted her napkin to her mouth. 'I don't know why you should suddenly decide to insult me. I really don't.'

She rose to her feet, her voluminous blue dress flickering static in the semi-darkness of the restaurant.

'I'm very sorry it should end like this, but I have no alternative but to leave.'

'It's your fault,' he said. 'You started it. And I am *definitely* not fatter than you. That's very obvious, if I may say so.'

He got up to seek out the proprietor and pay the bill. The evening had suddenly become a complete disaster, and must be ended. But as he tried to get to his feet, the awful realization hit him: he was stuck in his chair. He was completely wedged in.

He wiggled his hips, and then tried once more, but again with the same result. He was stuck between the wooden arms of the chair and each movement only seemed to make the fit even tighter and less yielding.

She had noticed what had happened and was staring at him triumphantly from the other side of the table. 'There you are!' she said. 'That proves it. I was right!'

He snorted angrily, and wriggled again. Now the proprietor had seen what was happening and rushed to his side.

'I'm terribly sorry, sir,' he said. 'I shall get you free. Do not worry.'

He bent down and began to tug at the wooden struts which held the top part of the chair together. He tugged sharply and there was a cracking sound. One of the struts came away.

'There we are,' he said. 'If I get a few more of these out, then you'll be able to release yourself. I am so sorry about this!'

She watched as the proprietor struggled. The real nature of the emergency had changed the situation somewhat, and she felt that she could not storm out now, as she had planned. She felt some sympathy for Edgar, even if he had insulted her. He did not deserve this embarrassment, this humiliation.

'I'm getting there,' said the proprietor, crouched down, tugging at a piece of wood. 'Perhaps this is a good advertisement for my food! Perhaps if everybody saw fat people like you coming in here and eating so well that they got stuck, then they'd know how good the food is!'

She drew in her breath sharply. 'How dare you!' she hissed. 'How dare you talk about us like that.'

Edgar was equally annoyed, and his heart gave a leap of pleasure when he saw her step forward and give the proprietor a sharp push. He was not expecting it, and he fell over, letting go of the strut of wood on which he had been tugging.

'Edgar,' she said. 'Get up and try to walk with that chair. We shouldn't spend a further second in this place.'

He leant forward and pushed himself up, the chair still firmly wedged about him. Then, bent double, he waddled out of the restaurant, with Nina close behind him.

The proprietor picked himself up off the floor and looked at the waiter. '*Ma, che cos'ho detto?*' he said. '*Che cos'ho fatto? Che cos'è successo a quei grassoni?*' (What did I say, I ask you! What am I meant to have done? What's going on with these well-upholstered people?)

The waiter said nothing. He had not understood a vital part of the exchange and it seemed to him that the whole situation was utterly opaque.

Outside, it was a warm summer night. There were few people in the street to stare at him, and even those who were making their way home at that hour hardly noticed the sight of a large woman with an equally large, or possibly even larger man at her side, the man half-seated in a chair.

'Sit down,' she said. 'Sit down on the chair. You'll be more comfortable. A taxi is bound to go past soon.'

So he sat down, relieved to get the weight of the chair off him.

He looked up at her. 'I'm terribly sorry I was inadvertently rude in there. I really wasn't thinking.'

She smiled. 'And I'm sorry too. It was thoughtless of me. I hope you'll forget all about it.'

'Of course,' he said.

Then they waited in silence. Somewhere, in a flat in the narrow tenemental street, a record was being played; of a fine tenor voice.

'Listen,' she said. 'Just listen!'

'How wonderful,' he said. 'How wonderful.'

Then he patted his knee. 'Why don't you sit down,' he said. 'We can sit here listening to that gorgeous sound until a taxi comes.'

She smiled at him. Why not? It had been a fine romantic evening, apart from the one incident. She liked him.

Perhaps they could face the indignities of the world together. Why not?

She adjusted her dress and lowered herself gently onto his knee.

Then the chair-legs broke.

THE POTATO THAT NEVER WAS

Fiona Pattison

The day I find The Potato That Never Was, you have to make do with fewer chips than usual. When I first feel at it with my cold wet hands in the soily water, I think I must be wrong.

'Chips tonight, is it?' you say, when you see me sitting, potato-faced, on the kitchen floor, holding it.

'Looks like it,' I say, scraping it with my fingernail, and blowing a bit of muck off it.

You reach down for me, and feather my hair a bit.

'See you then, chicken,' you say, and chuck me under the chin. I give you a peck.

When you've gone, I try to forget I've ever seen it. I try to forget that when I dropped it, it didn't thud or bounce, it clinked and just sat there. I dry it on a towel, and hide it inside a pan inside a bigger pan, right at the back of the dust of the kitchen cupboard, the one with the slidey orange door. But, standing at the sink again, I can still see it, looking up at me with its blind potato eyes. I find I'm staring, unseeing, looking through it, to something else. When I come back, it's to see that round the edges of the sink is a lace collar of bubbles, greasy as the white frill on fried eggs. And on the should-be silver of the taps, green is growing. The windows need cleaning. My fingers are zebra-striped and fat red, disintegrating.

My belly against the sink feels fat, as if there's something in there that shouldn't be, or something in there that didn't used to be, or something like new bread, still rising. I undo my zip, and pull my jumper down over my belly. That feels better. My skin's stretched, tighter than usual, as if it's making room for something, something that wants to come out, but can't, or won't.

Maybe I'm eating too much, I think, buttering another slice of bread, then scattering some of the crumbs out of the window, in case the birds come. I snack at some sesame seeds and bits of bacon, and listen to people going by, outside and out on the landing. Some neighbours pass.

'He's worse than he was,' I hear one of them say as they pass our door, the one without a name on.

'It's since he started stuffing that fat bird,' the other one says, and they both laugh.

I put the kettle on again, and turn the hoover on, and drive it at walls until they've gone.

When I've hoovered up, I go and sit in the other room, by the window, and, even though it's early, I open a bottle of wine. Then I open the window. Outside, down there, children are playing, and women are pushing prams by. A black dog's red tongue is panting in the gutter. I get the window open wide, and sit on the sill, and dangle my legs high above the street. I sip my wine, which is not wise this high up. I pour another glass, finish it, cry a bit, get dizzy, dry my eyes, and get down to open another bottle, while I'm waiting. I open the bottle, open the window a bit further, and settle back down onto my sill, and swing my legs, and lean against nothingness, and start to feel a bit sleepy.

Then you're back. The door slams. Seeing me by the window, so high, you think I'm trying to fly. It's an easy mistake to make.

'You're too young to fly,' you say.

Folding my arms behind my back, like chicken's wings, you make a neat parcel of me, so I'm all tucked up and in, firmly. And, now we're together again, I can't think of anything except your cock and your kisses. I get that taste of high in my mouth, like I've bitten a boiled sweet, or my tongue, and I don't care which.

'You're cold,' you say, thinking that's why I'm shivering. So, taking your chance while I'm heavy, you lift me up, and carry me across the room. I think you might only be trying to warm me, when you turn the oven on, and open the door, and put me in it, and slam the door, and leave me in it, and go for another pint, and forget the time.

It's hot. It's so hot in the oven that I'm cooked. I'm changed, slowly, stage by stage, from one thing to another. I can't move.

I think you put your hand on my arse, and, skilful as a vet up a cow, pulled out the important bits of me, and gave them to the cat to eat. Then stuffed me full of things I found irrelevant – sage, onions, and bread – things that didn't help me breathe again. You stuffed me till I felt so full, I thought I might explode myself all over you, surprising as a gangster's birthday cake. And I let you. Because I felt so empty, I let you put all sorts of stuff in me – eyes and hands and hearts and cocks and babies' lockets – and now I'm sitting wondering what they'll cook into.

Patting me, satisfied I looked the right shape, you slid me in. And what can I say? I opened my back legs to you. I let you stuff me till I was too fat to fly.

Now, I'm helpless as a chicken, my arms and legs trussed, as I'm cooked from raw to roast to ready. Just when I think I can't stand any more, you stick something sharp – a fork or a knife – between my shoulderblades, and say, 'That'll do.'

Out of my arsehole, soft, fur-grey smoke unfurls. I think I'm burning.

Taking me out of the oven, you pick up a big knife. You split me in half, cross-section me, starting at the fold of me, right between my legs. The two halves of me fall, clean as wood does, or potato chips. It's only taken one movement to do it.

I'm waiting. What is it you're looking for? You inspect each cross-section, I can see, looking at how things are put together. Are you looking for something you think you've lost? Do you expect to find it, nesting precious as an egg, in some heart of me? You crouch down and feel at me, efficient as a doctor, knowing just where to look. I feel at you feeling at me, unfamiliar as a doctor, looking for something familiar, or unfamiliar, or anything, to get hold of, so you can say you understand.

If I could have done, I would have chopped at you until you fell in chips, starchy-clean and powdery. I would have divided you white as firewood. I would have sizzled you into hot fat, and watched you, until you floated to the surface, until the chip fat gave me a round of applause.

But you were The Potato That Never Was. I broke two knives on you. I broke a window with you, trying to hurt you. I bruised my hand hitting you.

I shiver and look down at myself. My bare arms and legs are still white, not basted or frazzled. The hairs are standing up on them, which they would be. I pull myself together. I can still get up, so I do, and I leave you lying there, innocent as a stone.

SAND

Felicity Carver

The second night the quarrelling began again, the two voices clearly audible through the thin ceiling.

'Stop it, no, you're hurting. Please, no.'

'Don't give me that, girl, don't. Come on.' Followed by crying and the slap of bare feet on the floor above.

For God's sake leave her alone, Gemma thought, surprised at her own surge of anger. She tried to turn over, but Jon's arm had fallen like an anchor rope across her chest and she did not want to wake him. He was the kind of person whose limbs always seemed to be left about for people to blunder into, like a sea anemone extending tentacles, except that they used theirs for attracting prey. But that had been how they had met, she had fallen over him at Sheila's party.

'Their fighting sounds so awful,' Gemma complained at breakfast in the cramped dining room of the *pension*.

'Don't listen.'

'I can't not somehow.'

'It's their problem. Which ones do you think they are?' Speculation lit up Jon's face and his eyes moved over the different people. 'My money's on those two; looks as though he'd need his oats, got that glint in his eye.'

The man was dark and stocky, built like a footballer, with strong thighs protruding from the cut-off jeans he used as shorts, and a profusion of black curls covering his legs. His hair was slicked back into a central parting like in a photo from an old fashion magazine, and the way he carried himself had the arrogance of an athlete. The girl with him was smiling secretly to herself. Her long blonde hair was cut rather raggedly, giving her a waif-like look, though the hands that broke the roll into pieces were strong and capable, like a violin player's.

'They don't look right,' Gemma said.

'Guilt,' Jon said later, sprawling on the sand. 'You're happier feeling guilty, aren't you. I don't feel it, why do you?'

Gemma was annoyed by his percipience. 'It's wrong.'

'It doesn't matter. Nothing to do with us,' he said.

'No.'

But even when they returned in the early evening after swimming and he lay with his hand on her spine and she tasted the salt on his skin she could not forget. She felt infected by someone else's unhappiness; personal ecstasy no longer seemed possible with the counterpoint of the relationship above them. Gemma wept, her face streaming.

'For heaven's sake. We're on holiday,' Jon said.

'It's like being haunted. They're laying siege. It's a battle up there.'

'But it can't be, they look all right in the morning.'

'Perhaps she's too afraid to look otherwise.' The crying at night was like a child's, the same hiccoughing choke, the sniffing.

'Why does it have to be war?' she asked him at dinner, noticing the strong lines of his throat reddened by the sun.

'It doesn't. We prove that, don't we.' He took her hand across the table and rubbed the skin inside the wrist and she shuddered in pleasure as he knew she would.

'He likes to win, that's all,' said Jon. 'And maybe it's what she needs.' Gemma recognized an echo of pub talk, fists raised, with grunts of sound to express the indescribable.

'No one needs that.'

'Something about her,' said Jon. 'Could go for her myself. That sulky look.'

Petulant, Gemma thought next day, watching water glisten off the bony face, the mouth drooping slightly while the blue eyes glanced along the beach, looking at Jon lying on his face with the white mark where his swimming trunks normally reached showing against his tanned back. Gemma sat in the shade of the parasol, but the girl still lay in the sun, ignoring her burned shoulders. A towel over her back was the only concession; it lay like a flag across a body, under the sand that scattered in the afternoon breeze, grains running bleached through the gaps between chairs. Sand was everywhere, in the white folds of the sheet, on the floor, running from clothes and feet as if measuring time.

The girl's hair was sand-coloured; there were small freckles on her legs and the new skin on her shoulders gleamed, pink like a cat's tongue.

Gemma woke suddenly, her face hot against the bolster which passed for a pillow. Jon was lying without any covering, curled round, his hair falling over his face. A heavy scent, mimosa or bougainvillaea, gave the air an oppressive, physical quality.

A thump and a whine came from above; the hair on Gemma's neck cringed and she buried her face in the ancient smell of the bolster, inhaling dust and old emotions. In the thin wail she recognized an atavistic fear of her own and felt disoriented, as if the swell of the sunlit water still carried her, floating and weightless. An old fear from days when her father had shouted at her mother, drink in the colour of his face and in the shame of his eyes in the morning while the woman clutched a stiff arm, shocked and silent. And Gemma hating, yet too afraid to complain. They held him back, he said, he could have been, he might have done; a whole range of unkept promises she and her mother owed him. As soon as she was old enough Gemma had left, taking off to a new job one Friday, away from the loser's strength, its own contradiction. You must come, leave him, why not, she had said in desperation. But her mother had never gone, staying because she did not know how to leave, and anyway defiance meant being alone.

'Come and meet Bart and Rosie.' Jon waved at Gemma from the table by the bar.

But I can't, she thought in panic, except that there was no way to avoid it. Jon often attached himself to people at a moment's notice, like a stray dog.

'Knew you were English,' they said. 'Good place, isn't it.' And Bart picked up the bottle and poured a glass of wine for Gemma, pushing it across the metal surface. A harsh confidence came from him like the glare of the sea at midday. She was aware of the smell of suntan oil and beer and was afraid to look at his face in case he could read what she thought of him.

The wine tasted of earth.

The first time she had tasted earth had been as a child, after seeing birds with soil on their beaks from pecking at the grass, and thinking that must be what they ate. Seeking some magic that might allow her to learn to fly and escape from the anger that swarmed indoors, she had scraped a small handful from a bare patch of ground and pressed it into her mouth. Although the metallic grittiness had been surprisingly harsh against her tongue, even painful, drawing blood from a scratched gum so that salt mixed with the dissolving soil, there had been a curious satisfaction in the hurt as if it assuaged some previously unrecognized hunger. The new scraping taste in the softness of her cheek held a promise of other, different experiences and obliterated temporarily the fear of what she might find later at home. Even after she had realized that she would never fly, she had still found the granular sensation strangely comforting. But the sand that penetrated everything here, even her toothbrush, was not the same.

'I hope we don't disturb you at all,' said Bart.

'Oh no,' Gemma said, too swiftly. Bart and Rosie looked at each other and grinned. Gemma blushed. Bart's lips curved and the chair tilted as he swung his head back, laughing. His amusement was irreverent, there was something pagan about him. But then what was the girl? Pink and sunburned, perhaps she welcomed pain; there was no sign of tears in the daylight. If it was the same voice that complained at night, just enough to pierce Gemma's level of consciousness, forcing her to listen to the disharmony, why did the girl stay, what kept her? Jon was here because Gemma had organized everything, but she knew that he could just as easily have gone with someone else. Choose what you want, be my guest, I don't mind, he had said when she suggested the trip, and she had kissed him and said it would be so marvellous to get away, to be abroad, as if they would be different there, brochure-like people, always smiling, glowing, tanned and healthy. And he had come, she had him to herself for once, there were no threats; at home there were always others anxious to displace her. The holiday was for the two of them alone, no one else.

Trying to build a past for the future she hoped they would have, Gemma took photographs of Jon standing against the castle on the hill, and even persuaded some unsuspecting dark-eyed boy to take their picture down by the pier, as if something so tangible would link them for ever. She dressed for him too in the clothes she had bought, a new white shirt that she threw round her shoulders casually, knowing it was far too expensive to waste by getting it wet or stained; enjoying the extravagance balanced against her normal thrift. Jon did not mind about money, he said artists couldn't afford to. It was one of his casual jokes, an attempt to excuse the fact that he lived partly off her. On days of self-doubt, when she looked at herself critically in the mirror, she wondered why else he stayed.

The bruises were like a badge or a ribbon from some distant campaign, worn to remind, not hidden by the shirt which had been allowed to fall open.

'Why don't you leave him?' Gemma couldn't stay silent any more.

'You don't understand. I mean, I know he cares, he wouldn't do it otherwise. If I wasn't important to him.'

Gemma was left staring out to sea, watching a windsurfer balance precariously on his board, then fall as the sail deflated. She hadn't the courage to ask Jon if she was important to him, or the other questions at the back of her mind: when would they settle, when could she have a child, when would talking of such things not scare him away.

When Gemma met Bart on the stairs or in the narrow passage she felt a challenge in the way he appeared to move courteously out of the way yet still brushed against her. But Jon and Rosie got on well, teasing each other with the familiarity of a brother and sister. Rosie called Jon a scrawny brute, a conceited yuppie, a pseud, until he grabbed her towel and threw it down the beach and she scattered sand towards him and they laughed. When Gemma joined in they stopped at once and she was left out of the game.

'Why don't you like me?' Bart asked once in the cool darkness of the hallway.

Gemma felt trapped. 'I never said I didn't.'

'No, you don't have to.' An easy smile, the broad blue eyes regarding her gently. 'Your hackles go up every time I appear.'

'The walls are dead thin, aren't they,' she said.

'We don't hear much,' he said, and she flushed at the implied criticism. 'Why do you bother with him?'

'Why not?' she said defensively.

In the shadows he looked much browner, still wearing the faded denim, the fringes growing longer as the threads unravelled.

'If you like him, tell him to keep away from Rosie, will you?'

'There's nothing in it.' She wanted to believe he was wrong.

'Then he won't get hurt. And with you, anything in that?'

'Of course.'

'So long as you're happy?'

The raised eyebrows mocked her. Gemma turned away, irritated, hearing his bare feet scuffing the steps. Why had he told her and not Jon? Half an hour later, when Bart spread out his towel after swimming and stretched out on the sand beside Rosie, Gemma listened for argument, but the voices had dropped, now there were only the vibrations drumming on her ear like some curious distant music, mixing with the cries of children and an insistent beat from the bar loudspeakers. She was becoming obsessed; she wanted to know what it was that made them lie so close beside each other on the beach, their self-absorption so evident that people avoided them, keeping a distance as if their intensity required more privacy than others'. Inside, lying in the warm darkness, she still saw the sleek wet figures on the sand, and pleaded sunburn as an excuse when Jon began to kiss her neck, his usual prelude. He was gentle and offered to rub on lotion and she found herself crying again later in the thick darkness, which was like some strange sea that washed over her mind, because she was envious and also afraid.

On Gemma and Jon's last night, all four of them ate together in the small restaurant by the pier which they thought of as their discovery, and which would be rediscovered by others all summer. Jon had been eager for company and somewhere between the steps and the sea the assumption that they would all go together became inevitable. Rosie leaned over the table, giggling, while Jon mispronounced the names on the menu, choosing a fish that translated as mullet. Gemma hardly spoke, feeling curiously uninvolved. It wasn't until she caught Bart's eye unexpectedly that she broke into the conversation, annoyed by her own lack of assurance. When eventually they got up to leave, following coffee and some obscure liqueur that tasted to Gemma of petrol, Rosie hugged Jon in a moment of fleeting sentiment, her strong hands playing his spine like a violin. Gemma walked out into the darkness which was warm on her shoulders, and Bart followed her, stubbing out his cigarette with his bare feet on the concrete.

'Doesn't that hurt?'

'Sometimes.'

She hadn't expected him to admit to pain, assuming he inflicted it unawares.

'You've still got something against me,' he said.

'You hurt people.'

He shrugged. 'And how about him?' He indicated the others, following slowly, a linked silhouette. 'Doesn't that hurt you?'

'It doesn't mean anything,' she said hopefully.

'I would never let anyone else hurt her.' He was standing with his arms crossed, aggressive in the multicoloured darkness of the pier. 'I'd kill them.'

He cares, the girl had said. That's why. She remembered her mother's refusal to listen to Gemma's demands that she should leave, the way she shook her head repeatedly as if gesture was the only clear language. And had her father cared, was that why her mother had stayed, recognizing that it could only happen to her? Was some kind of need expressed in acceptance of the hurt? He would never have had the strength to hurt anyone else, because no one else would have cared about the ineffectual blows, the attempts to pay life back for the fear that he might never be anything more; seeing his impoverished reflection mirrored in their disappointed faces.

She shivered in the breeze from the sea, and Bart offered her his sweatshirt, but she refused because she would not admit to wanting anything from him.

*   *   *

'I can't stand it,' she said later, 'not tonight, not our last night,' which was to have been something to remember, something to have and to hold. But the sound that came from upstairs defeated any attempts at oblivion.

A crash and then swearing followed and feet stamped across the floor. Gemma remembered other noises, a plate flying and her mother ducking, white-faced as a clown, while the scar where it tore the paper was left for days as a reminder. And then coming back from school one day Gemma found the wall re-papered, as if covering the mark would hide the feelings that had led to it.

Clutching Jon's beachrobe round her because it offered more protection, she ran flat-footed up the narrow stair and hammered on the door. The noises stopped and she knocked again.

'What is it?'

He had a towel wrapped round his waist, his feet were splayed out wide on the boards at the edge of the room and he wiped his face with his hand.

'For God's sake stop it.' She was rigid with indignation, hands clenched. 'None of us can sleep.'

'Some of us don't want to,' he said.

Regretting the impulse that had taken her up there, she wanted to say something devastating, but found herself staring instead at the girl who appeared behind him, her hands on his shoulders, dark shapes of painted nails like warning pennants on the brown skin.

'Do you want to join us?' The teeth were very white in the dark doorway. He was shaking with badly suppressed laughter, and the girl began to smile too.

Gemma turned and walked blindly to the end of the passage, hearing the door slam and the stifled comment, the wild mockery. In panic she began to plunge down the stairs, holding her hands over her ears, shutting out the noise, the fear pounding inside her head, the knowledge that she had almost accepted sending her running back to Jon and the stifling warmth of their small room.

Next morning she stood on the ferry and gazed at the weed and debris washing against the harbour wall, inhaling the scent of decaying fruit and rotting fish and somewhere beyond it a hint of thyme from the hill above. Then, feeling sick as the ferry rounded the cliff and began to buck through the waves, she staggered along the deck, clutching the rail, looking for shelter. As she clambered down the ladder the boat shifted and she fell, catching the side of her face against a curved strut that supported the deck above. In the cramped lavatory with its cracked basin, she swallowed dry-mouthed a travel sickness pill and splashed water against her face, examining the damage. A slight stiffness warned of swelling; holding the wet cold handkerchief against it, she saw the beginning of a bruise under the fringe of dark hair. Gemma put the handkerchief back in her bag, and combed her hair to one side so that the mark would show.

'Here,' Jon said, slopping over the pitching deck in the sandals which fell off his heels at each step. 'I bought you a glass of wine, it might help. What have you done to your face?' he asked, drinking. 'Everyone'll think I'm like Bart.'

'Yes,' she said, taking the wine, sensing the same rumour of soil she had detected before, and she forgot the strong hands fingering Jon's back and the undeveloped photos of the time they had never had, and tasted the freshness of moist earth, the roughness of grit against her teeth, darkness and damp, away from the swell of the sea and diamond-hard grains of sand and the brilliant light, and felt again that strange childhood satisfaction.

AN APT CONCEIT

Alison Armstrong

1. FIRST SITTING: Portraying Dr Krabbe

How can I portray this man? A man with a face eaten by the vilest of diseases, yet who must be handsome, or I'm dead? A man with a fish for a mouth and the arse of a plucked chicken for a nose? I, who must paint for a living, must paint lies – but even lies need substance. I cannot paint thin air.

He sits, waiting; that head of monsters propped on the writs and affidavits that emerge at his neck instead of linen. Soon, the girl he calls his niece will enter with a jug of cold wine and one cup. She will embrace him and the documents will crack. She is no more than seventeen, the little witch. She is springtime, apart from her breasts, which are Autumn's pulpy apples. She should not be given to that stinking flesh – whose beady chicken's eye stares at my hat and cloak which lie crumpled near the door. I should be sketching, but my hand can barely grip the charcoal. This is a duel, a tennis match, in which the body and mind have colluded with the opponent's. I know why he's staring at my hat and cloak. He's cross-examining.

This room is full of flies. They are settling on the fruit and the cold meats that have been left beside him. Without taking his eye from my cloak, he picks a grape, or nips off a morsel of beef or chicken breast between finger and thumb. His hands are clusters of gnawed drumsticks which, (thank God), I do not have to paint.

He has just eaten a fly. He held it and swallowed it as

if it were a raisin. My right hand has turned to stone, but his hand, with its fingerbones protruding, is still dextrous. The skin of his niece is bone-scratched and she conceals these wounds with ointments. I saw these wounds, when she met me at the front door. My eyes are trained to penetrate deceits.

I attempt a curve; the dome of his head in that black caul. He wears it to hide the hole where his ear should be. Whores once whispered in that ear, as they slowly nibbled it away.

The dome I have drawn would fit the elongated skull of a Negro. I draw men I can't see. Until today, God was in my eye and my right hand, but He has abandoned me. He abandoned me on the threshold of this house and I am like my cloak: crumpled. I need to find stuffing from somewhere, or I will not earn a penny. He wanted to engage me at an hourly rate, but I said that wouldn't work. But in his heart he's still paying good money for this solitary black man's dome.

(Heart? *Heart?* If it's there, it's a lumpy turd shat by the Devil.)

He is not a man. He is a demon that jumped in when God departed from me. Azazael, the smelly one. Beelzebub – eating flies to pass maggots, while he grows rich sending witches to Hell. Chief Prosecutor he is, in this fair city, and no Minister or City Father has ever seen him as I see him now.

When he coughs, or farts, the midden-pile of his being shivers, as if ready to fall apart. Each cough, or fart, is a dry hicuppy wheeze that smells of fish and heartshit. It is the smell of the disease, and Hell. I could paint what I see and name it 'Pox', but I still have to paint a young Jove, or a Solomon.

He sucks me; sucks my talents from my cloak. In shameful dreams I have been visited by his niece but *he* was the one at work below. He does not leave the room to piss, but performs this operation in front of me. A bowl has been left for this purpose, and he barely has to stand. I can see nothing on account of his baggy breeches, but he does not even say 'Excuse me.' He just returns to sitting and eating.

His water is reddish and smells high. Like vinegar on salad it mingles with the fartcoughs and the smell of the food. If the plague has a workshop, it is in this room. All the windows are shut and a fire is dying in the grate. It could be a beautiful room – a chamber for the niece, perhaps – but it is bare and dusty and the plasterwork around the fireplace is cracked. The wall-plaster is cracked, too. Each crack is a spindly leg where the flies breed, and the bold mice wait in corners for dropped food. But his mouldy claws never drop a morsel.

I have shaded the caul. I did not mean to, but it became a shape to toy with as I sat. My shading is childish; it even ventures over the outline in places. I want to draw the face, but I hold back because such devils must not be seen on this earth . . . Be industrious. The niece has returned with the chilled wine and I do not want her to see . . .

'Is that *all*?'

She will bring me to grief, with her complaining. Those pulpy apples heave with her scorn and the pressure of leaning over me. I cannot ignore them because they heave next to my face.

'My hand is stiff,' I tell her. 'I need to do a few – er – exercises before I start work.' Her concealing ointment smells of musk and the stiffness in my right hand becomes *nothing* against the stiffness of my snake. I am afraid it will burn my breeches, in its desire for a hole.

'*Exercises!*' she squeals. 'You keep uncle here for your *exercises!*' And she snatches my work and gambolls towards that mass of dead flesh as if she were carrying a posy of flowers. 'Uncle! uncle!' she trills. 'Look what the man has done.'

(I think she is simpleminded. Apart from the commonest

sort, young women have low voices and keep their opinions to themselves.)

Uncle takes his eye from my cloak and looks at my drawing. He studies it for a long time and as he does so, butterflies frolic in my gut. Then he speaks, dry as the parchment that stuffs him. 'Not very impressive,' he admonishes my cloak, my crumpled self.

'Well . . . ,' I stammer. (How do you address a witchburner? Sir? Your Honour? My Lord?) 'Well, My Lord, I . . . I sometimes find it hard . . .'

(The niece giggles. Damn her to Hell if she isn't going there already.)

'. . . to . . . to see the truth when its vessel is in front of me.'

The fingerbones roll and unroll a sliver of beef fat. I will have to explain myself better, which will be difficult because I am a painter. I do not flatter with words. 'Philosophy,' I begin, 'says that we must imitate the Eternal. If we do not – if we look to the shadows that surround us – our labour is a poor and worthless sham.' I have never seen the Eternal, and those who have, could not paint a tavern sign because they are mad. I have the thread of *something* in this pedantry, that may lead me out of this plague-pit. I am no logician, so I can only follow where it goes.

The fishmouth belches. 'Meaning?' it croaks.

'While I sit here I am blind to your spirit,' says the angel who handed me this thread. 'Your form is a manly one, but your spirit is the sword of God. It is His anger, His justice, and, for the good people of this town, His infinite compassion.'

A bead of water is squeezed from the chicken's eye, and rolls down the raw cheek. Niece wipes it carefully, and as she looks up from her task, she smiles – not at him, at *me*. Then – being simpleminded, not vulgar – she winks. 'I must leave,' says my angel to Dr Krabbe, 'so I can discover your spirit.' As I speak, I take up my cloak and spring to the door. Once I am free of devils and this plague air, I will work again. But at my back I hear, 'Where are you going?' and I am pursued by foul eructations. The door is locked, and Niece has kept the key in her bodice. She has closed in on me, musk-smelling; and the key she offers yet withholds will be warm and greasy and musk-smelling too. She holds the key in her right hand. In her left hand she holds my pot of charcoals, and she has my drawing rolled up under her arm. 'What's Uncle's spirit *really* like?' she whispers, fingering the key.

'An angel with a sword,' I reply, also in a low voice.

'Young?'

'Yes.'

Her eyes widen. We are so close, I can examine the wounds made by her uncle's bones. There is one on her cheek and two or three across her breasts: he only cuts into deep flesh. The musk perfume bleeds from the depths of these gashes, and fills my head. I add, almost silently so I breathe upon her, 'Like you, he is very beautiful.'

She opens the door with that greasy key. She is my Ariadne. She tries to return my charcoals and paper, but I have no use for them and as I press the charcoals back into her hand, I seal her fingers with a kiss, which is a small price to pay for my deliverance. 'My studio,' I murmur. 'Top of the brick building, opposite the clock tower.'

'Mmmm.' Her very assent breathes musk, and sweet corruption. I have not fixed a time. I will expect her whenever she can get away.

Women's hearts are their souls. I will pray for hers, caught in the spikes of that old flycatcher. Once I am out of here I will breathe pure air and God will return to my soul. And to my right hand.

2. IN THE STUDIO: Two Days Later

'Ariadne!'

Her real name is Eloise, but I have rechristened her.

'Ariadne! Try not to wriggle.'

'I've got an itch . . .'

I am not surprised. Despite the musk, her intimate parts smell of bad lettuce and I was unable to go through with it. I did not hurt her feelings: I explained it would have been the wrong thing to do to her uncle's Spirit – which she depicts perfectly. She looks boyish in my bright armour, with her short, golden, curly hair. She says that her hair was cut recently because she had a fever. At her feet is coiled the Serpent – a cunning arrangement of pillows and rolled blankets because I cannot, and will not, seek the Eternal. Philosophy can say what it likes.

'Ariadne – have you ever seen a crocodile?'

'What's that?'

'You're killing one.'

A man I know has been to Africa and has seen these monsters spawning from the mud. He brought back the jaws of one, which he saw bite a man in half. I have used these jaws – which are fearsome – many times, but they can be added later. The bright armour belonged to my grandfather, who fought in the armies of the Turk. The breastplate was worn at the Fall of Constantinople, which impresses Ariadne deeply. If she were a man, she says, she would fight for the Turk.

'Why not for Christendom?' I ask. In reply, she makes a blowing noise with her lips and gives me a bald, insolent stare. She is a strange child. I still think she is simple-minded, but only if she is viewed through a mirror, with the glass tilted a certain way.

'Yeah – why not?' leers a voice from the shadows. Manfred! Manfred – who primes my canvas so it flaps like a wet sail. Manfred – who spills linseed oil when the agents of Princes are visiting my studio. Manfred – who I almost caught with his fingers in Ariadne's wounds. She was changing into her armour, and I only saw the exchange through a very dirty mirror, so I cannot be *sure*. I am waiting for her to complain, then I can kick him out the door, then down the stairway Until I saw that quintessence of rot two days ago, Manfred was my image of malignity. He is just sixteen, but his hair is thinning and there is barely a tooth in his head. He wanted to be apprenticed to a gunsmith, but his mother – may God forgive her! – opposed the idea.

'Manfred . . .' In a voice that would shame a choir of angels, Ariadne tells Manfred what to do with his plaything. Knowing Manfred, he will try it.

'Could you move the helmet forward, Ariadne?' I request.

Grandfather's helmet is tucked under her left arm. It was a preposterous thing covered in plumes, until I plucked it. I gave Manfred the plumes: a companion of his breeds fighting cocks and likes to enhance their tail feathers before a match. Manfred will never be a painter because he cannot *translate*. He does not look at Ariadne and see Truth vanquishing Error. He sees a girl prodding a blanket roll with a wooden sword. 'Thought you were doing the old Prosecutor,' he hissed at me when Ariadne walked in this morning.

'I am,' I hissed back – although I do not have to explain myself. 'Allegorically.'

'Ah.' He did not understand the word, but he was grinning slyly as he ground my pigment. I would love to lock him in that room, with the Krabbe visage and the flies to contemplate. Manfred eats toadstools, so he can fight giant spiders from Hell. He would not be so brave against a true devil – whose image I now see whenever I close my eyes.

Looking in the mirror this morning I saw the gashes in Ariadne's flesh. They are like Christ's wounds in popish paintings; not bleeding, more like deep red mouths that do not impair beauty. I am painting the wound on her cheek as a gash received in battle with the Evil One.

'How is your uncle?' I ask, with great politeness. She smiles broadly – no doubt the word 'uncle' amuses her.

'He is well, and happy.' (Neither of these words fit.) She continues. 'I told him I was coming here and he laughed and said it was good because I'm the pretty one.'

Am I the only one who sees the horror? Perhaps I am drinking something strange – the juice of the toadstool squeezed into my wine. Manfred!

There is malignity in the very air of this town, but it resides in more exalted vessels than Manfred. I could not have him killed as a sorcerer, just because he disgusts me. He is supposed to practise drawing when he has nothing to do, but the only drawings I have seen are of his member, or toadstools. I have not seen him for a while, so he must be absorbed in something grubby . . . thinking of her lettucey, musky smell.

'I'm tired,' Ariadne wails. 'Can we stop now?' She is so assertive, yet so pliant. Women's characters are see-saws.

'One moment.' The hand grasping the sword is not quite correct. It needs more shading . . . there! 'You can rest now.'

She lets sword and helmet fall on the blankets, and comes to view my work. This time there is more to see than a dome. There is a figure, standing above a still headless dragon. Together, they form a pillar in a desert. They stand at the edge of a cliff, and beyond them, the dry landscape stretches out and ultimately mingles with the sky. The sky itself is neither blue, nor yellow, but a colour of subdued radiance; of mysteries concealed.

'What's that?' demands Ariadne. She sounds no more impressed than she was with my dome.

I tap my skull. 'It's somewhere inside here.'

'It isn't real, then?'

'It's as real as your uncle's angel.'

She looks perplexed and I cannot blame her. She is contemplating something that is, and is not. Sometimes we see a cloud that's dragonish, then it becomes a horse, or a fist, or a man asleep. 'Can I get changed?' she asks. 'Yes.' She came here in a simple townswoman's dress, with a veil across her face. She explained her simplicity by saying, 'I didn't want to bring a maid.' She refused to let me help with her undressing, yet I caught Manfred, and her, in the mirror . . .

'Shall I call Manfred, to help you?' I enquire, as she retires to the corner where all my models – except my paying subjects – change. To have Manfred as a rival, who is less fastidious than I, is absurd . . . I tried, when she lay down for me – God knows I tried. In the Prosecutor's house I could have . . . but not today. Her smell was bad. The glass bears her image, so she cannot be a witch; however, she saps my puissance.

She turns. 'No; it's your turn, this time.' She begins to worm out of a gauntlet. The old counterpane I installed as a screen is tossed back, over the cord that folds it. Manfred will see everything.

I help her to unbuckle, and the musk odour reaches me, as from a slowly opening casket. I want to kiss each wound, and suck forth that smell, but Manfred is watching us. 'Who did these?' I venture, when I have lingered on her face, her breasts.

She is confused. She blushes, and does not meet my eye. 'My kitten did them,' she says at last and steadies herself by laughing. 'You will have to see my kitten. He is like you – he wants to do so many things, but dare not. Come and see him before he grows big, and bolder . . . Now, where did you find all *these*?'

She is staring at my costume trunk. The lid is propped open and masks and fans and gold and silver lace softly breathe out old revelry. 'Geneva,' I tell her. 'The citizens are too Godly nowadays to wear such things.'

She pulls a face and starts tumbling the contents of my trunk. Eventually she hauls out a dress of sapphire velvet, embroidered with flowers and twisting tendrils in gold thread. It is a strange dress; old, and out of fashion, but very beautiful. Ariadne holds it against her and the tendrils become perfect echoes of her hair.

'Keep it.'

Her lips fall open slightly. 'Can I?'

I nod, sourly, in confirmation. In her excitement, Ariadne wants to leave my studio wearing the dress, but as this town might soon go the way of Geneva, I forbid it. I perform the office of a maid and help fasten her townswoman's dress, then I take the counterpane and wrap it around the velvet gown. Into this bundle I throw a mask, a pair of high-heeled slippers and a large, gaudy, gilt rosary. It might blast that filthy old uncle into a pox-laden stew.

'Can I go home, now?' She is standing so close to me, I think she wants to stay. I think she wants to try me again, and see me fail. Ripe apples, almost rotting. A year maybe, or even less, and her disease will show. I hand her the bundle and she balances it on her head, like a washerwoman. Once I close the door – and I am closing it behind her, now – all my desire, and therefore all my shame, will cease. I will be purposeful, and clean inside . . .

TEHEHEHEHEHE!

Manfred!

What in Heaven's name is he doing? He is stumbling and trampling on the roll of blankets and with the wooden sword is parrying the thrusts of his reflection. He cannot hold the sword properly because the spiders are tickling him without mercy.

'Manfred!'

He is at Hell's mouth, so he does not hear.

'Manfred – YOU ARE TOO NEAR MY PAINTING!'

'Sorry . . .' He totters off the blanket and presses his face against the mirror. I cannot tell what he thinks he sees. Then he steps back three or four paces. 'That . . .' he says, pointing at his reflection, 'that is Alexander. That is . . . CAESAR!'

'Caesar' is a lion's roar. Manfred's jaw hangs open and his eyes are blank and bright, like a beast's. Men are changing into animals, or malignant *things*, and I ought to leave this town, before it happens to me.

'Manfred' – my voice is not quite steady – 'this is nonsense. Caesar and Alexander do not live in my looking-glass.'

He blinks once, twice; then looks at me. His eyes are closer to their usual sunken muddiness. 'It isn't anything,' he pronounces. 'It's just me.'

Very good, Manfred. A little melancholy will suit, after such ecstasies, but you do not have to skulk. I am not going to give you a beating, although I should. You would be thrashed ten times over at the gunsmith's, where they would not suffer those sidelong glances of yours.

Do not sidle up to me. Do not paw my sleeve and do not think about whispering in my ear.

But you do. You can do all these things because my blood freezes me when you are close. 'Master,' you mutter. 'Did you think that girl was *nice*?'

Your lips are curled in a sly sneer. Why, Manfred? Did she not please *you*?

3. TRUTH VANQUISHING ERROR:
The Painting Revealed, Several Months Later

'An apt conceit,' says My Lord Provost, squinting upward. The phrase will not be of his own devising.

(Dr Krabbe has bestowed his spiritual likeness on our city, and with great ceremony Ariadne was hung today, in the Guildhall. She hangs amid portraits of wise and honourable men, whose warty faces show Time at work on our clay. But she isn't warty. She is Truth and – were it not for the gash I painted on her face – Perfect Beauty; and since she visited my studio I have failed to pleasure women. Even in my dreams I fail, as her musky ointment, and her rotting vegetable disease, pursue me there. But she is no witch. She is the niece of our Chief Prosecutor.)

'Many thanks,' say I, bowing to the Provost. He inclines slightly, in return. We are two black pecking crows: the larger crow (the Provost), entitled to the fatter worm. Every man assembled here is a crow or a cockroach – metamorphosed by his love of God. Our flesh smells evil when soberly wrapped: somehow, the stink was tolerable inside gaudy rags. We swamp this building and its bitterly fresh smell of new timber, and we swarm here to honour our Sword of Justice, Dr Krabbe.

The Doctor is in our midst, and Ariadne wheels the banquet of foul flesh around in a barrow. This flesh is festering – blooming before our eyes, yet the crows and the cockroaches still swarm . . . finding the holes left by his ears and chattering therein. How they love his spiritual likeness! How our city thanks him for his work!

He swallows them, like a scavenging cat. I cannot tell if the rules of digestion still apply. Does he have a stomach to receive them? Will they, whole or part-whole, crawl down his collapsing passages, and will *he*, now or at some later date, shit flatterers?

. . . Ariadne is indifferent to them. From behind the front slit of her long black cloak, gold gleams: the lascivious crucifix swings against her corrupted parts when she walks. Her face has been slashed, many times, by the affections of her uncle's hands, but, as before, no blood weeps from those wounds. Maybe it mingles with her ointment, and becomes solid. Once, I saw a painting of a slaughtered man, where the assassins had hacked flesh from his leg and his side, and yet he was clean, and pale, and beautiful.

She pokes her tongue at me, and winks.

'Fine girl,' says My Lord Provost, and beams. He sees nothing amiss, but I would take that barrow and pitch it into the maw of a volcano . . . I must not think such thoughts; as long as there is life in that barrow, they will be read. I am drinking my third glass, and must guard against folly. In the Kingdom of God Bacchus is humble, but he is Bacchus nonetheless.

The Provost sweats pork fat. Manfred has whispered to me that, on our city's behalf, he is to reward my skill by offering me the hand of his idiot half-sister. (The girl's wits were addled by the milk she sucked from her nurse.) If the Provost does offer me his sister, I will take her. An idiot girl will not realize I can no longer *do*.

How does Manfred know My Lord Provost's intent? After his companion was well nigh flayed for holding cock-fights on the Sabbath, Manfred improved – or, his malevolence turned subtle. Sometimes, his little black eyes – deeply set, like currants in dough – glitter with intelligence. When I painted the monster, Error's, head, the crocodile jaws kept snapping shut. Manfred held them open, by attaching the upper jaw to the end of the rolled blanket, with a piece of twine. Thus he created a fantastical beast whose head grew from its tail or its tail from its head.

Manfred is here today, working as a pot-boy. His presence makes this floor as brittle as ice on a winter pond. I must trust him, however, or he will be knavish until he dies.

All will be well, if I keep my breathing steady. But here he comes.

'Very apt,' The Provost repeats, tugging his eyes away from Ariadne. 'All-egor-ical.'

'Yes. That was my intention.'

Manfred is upon us, to fill our cups. He carries the jug on his shoulder, stooping like a humpback, until he is ready to pour.

'Wine?' He addresses The Provost, not me, which is a fine distinction of rank. The jug could be a head, tendered on a platter . . .

. . . but whose head?

The wine flows into The Provost's cup: an exact fountain

from the tilted jug. A good servant is a table or a chair –
his humanity does not push and shove. But *is* Manfred
good? Is anyone?

The Provost's cup is filled and he drinks deeply. Manfred
and I watch, and wait. 'Will there be anything more?'
Manfred finally asks. No 'Sir,' or 'My Lord,' although the
question is deferentially pitched.

'Yes,' says My Lord Provost. 'There will be something
more. Who's that girl over there?'

'She came with Dr Krabbe . . .' I start to caution.

'She's his niece,' Manfred interposes. 'He is looking to
find her a husband.'

The Provost emits a quiet, purring growl.

'Eighteen,' adds Manfred softly, and proceeds, hump-
backed, towards the unclaimed bride.

*. . . Ariadne. Your perfume would make a man fly but you would
nibble his nose away.* You are too good and too bad for a man
who smells of pork fat; who cannot see beneath your black
satin cloak or behind your boy-angel hair. You bend over
that offal you call Uncle, and exchange a kiss.

'What's your picture called again?' The Provost demands.

'Truth Vanquishing Error.'

The Provost belches. 'You've done that girl, haven't
you?'

Ariadne is beautiful. Manfred is spiderlike. He acts the
humpback again as he escorts Ariadne and she laughs, with
her hand resting on his free arm. Her laugh is false, female,
dumb – at one with the ointment that hides her wounds.
Neither fools me.

'So why did he paint you and not your uncle?' enquires
My Lord Provost, affably.

She giggles, 'I'm the handsome one.'

The Provost laughs heartily, although there is no
joke.

Manfred laughs, too.

'The Doctor is an excellent and Godfearing man,' The Provost admonishes when the laughter is dead.

'But not handsome,' says Ariadne.

'Not handsome,' agrees Manfred, sotto voce.

I have painted a lie about beauty and truth. Truth is full of warts, and worse. It is a heap of dirt, sucked dry by Ariadne's kiss. Bluebottles circle above this midden like the stars and the chicken eyes lie haphazardly – piercing my skull in two separate places. They have transfixed me through twelve months' motion and business, and only the force of gunpowder will blow them away.

'No – no, my dear,' wheezes The Provost, venturing an arm around Ariadne's waist, 'your uncle is a very excellent man and – and we need him very much in this town. You've heard about my sister, and the nurse's milk –'

'Yes,' says Ariadne. 'It's very sad.' In her black satin cloak, she slips away from the arm. 'Uncle says that Satan is ready with a big net to catch every soul in this town. Even the greatest, and the most devout.'

I would like to kick Manfred, but he stands just out of reach. I want to be sure he does not speak.

''Specially the greatest . . .' he mutters. O, sweet Jesus. That is a prayer, not a blasphemy. Manfred's little eyes have an infernal fire in their depths, which I did not notice when I took him on. He is exceeding the duties of a pot-boy, and we should not listen to him although his jug holds Greek Fire, not liquor. He wanted the gunsmith's, not my studio . . . 'Is it true,' he asks, humbly seeking enlightenment, 'that a woman who paints sees the devil in her looking-glass?'

In the space of a wink, Ariadne grows older and more sly. She laughs. 'Of course it's true –' and her tone hisses, 'you know it, you little vile toad.'

My Lord Provost blinks heavily, and stares at her complexion. 'What's a girl like you paint for?'

She blushes, and her blood quickens yet fails to break from its musky dungeon. 'I had a fever, and when I recovered I –'

(Manfred is watching her intently, and her eyebeams are trying to tug it all out. If I could prevent him with my gaze, I would, as she has endured sufficient hurt, from Krabbe-claws).

'I had blemishes, all red like so many mouths – or other places . . .' She drops her eyelids modestly.

My Lord Provost's fancy has never teemed with such multitudinous bliss. He is a small toothless dog faced with an entire roasted ox. In spite of his youth, Manfred can chew and digest, and his insalubrious parts relive their tryst in my studio. Both these men are beasts.

'You are perfect,' I assure her, gallantly. She needs some homage *in words*; otherwise her honour, and our dignity, would turn to dust.

'Thank you. You are kind.' She is ice, because I failed her. Her beauty is exquisite – riper than last year, because it is *turning*. Soon she will rot.

She has slipped her white hand into The Provost's greasy paw. 'You can take me back to my uncle,' she tells him, and her speech crowns a pig with lilies. Then she nods farewell and they return to the barrow; only My Lord Provost is not escorting *her*. She is leading him, by the snout.

'Do you see that?' Manfred asks softly, tapping his nose. I nod, musing upon the manifest beastliness of men. History speaks of our glory, but we fall. Is there nothing that will keep us on our feet?

Manfred's face is bisected by the extent of his grin. I frown on him severely. 'Explain yourself.'

With his free hand, Manfred outlines a large oval ass-ear, against his own head. 'She must've winked at you,' he remarks, 'Master.'

He can barely contain his laughter, so he thinks it politic to leave. He hoists his jug on his shoulder and lollops off, squat as a toad, agile as a spider, to quench more animal thirsts.

He will always be a mountebank.

ENTERTAINING DOROTHY

Iain Bain

I don't know these people. They are not my friends. Daddy made Janice bring them here. I've seen them all before, at the new school and out in the street but that doesn't make them my friends, does it? My friends would have come to the old house but I mustn't talk about there.

I got to choose who I wanted to come because it was my party, Daddy said, and I said I wanted Florence and I wanted a clown like on the telly.

'Wouldn't you like some other children, darling?' I knew Janice wanted me to say yes, so I said it, but it wasn't true. Are are lies wicked just the same, or are some more wicked than others? Mr Popo told lies. There's lies and there's just pretending and there's making a mistake. Mr Popo said that he was a clown from the circus, but Daddy told Janice that he was a clerical something. That's not a clown, is it? Mr Popo said we were going to have a good time.

I just wish I could just shut up sometimes. You work hard. You try to build a reputation, to be dependable. I'm good at my job, but these days, Christ, it's not enough. Still, I keep my head down and I don't give myself away. Then the office party, a few drinks and it's 'Look at me I'm Danny bloody Kaye.' I was doing the ventriloquist bit, trying to impress. And then big Gordon is all over me, all affability and large whiskies. Next thing I'm down in that big Legoland villa of his – Mr poxy Popo. I was telling him it was just for a laugh and I couldn't do crowds and specially not crowds of kids. It was like trying to tell an avalanche to kindly go back up the mountain. I just wish I could keep my mouth shut, so I do.

They said that it was my day and they said that all they wanted in the world was to make me happy. The thing about grown-ups is that they don't tell you everything, so you don't understand. It's hard when you don't understand. When I'm a grown-up and I understand everything I'm going to explain it to the children.

The suit was ridiculous and I felt such a sad case in it. The nose was cheap plastic and it hurt like hell. No proper shoes; I was wearing brown Hush Puppies, for God's sake. I tried.

'Gordon, look . . . Gordon, can't we . . . ?'

He didn't give me a chance. A healthy measure of Scotch courage and I was on a wee platform in the front room. It wasn't The Palladium but it was no less terrifying, let me tell you. There were about a dozen of them all looking up at me. They seemed pretty excited apart from wee Dorothy. Funny one that; just sat there with her doll. Anyway, I give it a big 'Hello boys and girls. I'm Mr Popo the clown,' and we're off. I did a daft wee song to get them going, then a bit of falling about and some jokes before my big finale. It was okay once I got started. Could have been worse.

The man's teeth were bad and he smelt funny, a bit like Janice's dressing table and Daddy after the golf club. His nose wasn't real. I don't mean like when Daddy says 'That traffic wasn't real, Janice.' It didn't look like skin. He was supposed to be a clown, but he wasn't like a clown, not really. It was okay when he was up on the platform, but then he came down. I didn't want him to come any closer but he did. He came right across the room, not looking at anybody but me. He was sweating and he looked scared. Then he was standing right in front of me and he said, 'You're Dorothy, aren't you?' And I said yes. Why did he have to talk so loud? Why did everyone have to hear? That wasn't nice. Next he said, 'And who's this?' I said, 'Florence.' Then it happened.

Sometimes I look in the mirror and I think you pitiful bastard. Who do you think you are? What are you doing here? Some people make you think they know what it's all about. They don't. None of us do. I saw big Gordon with his wee girl. He was jollying her along, talking about the party and that. The wee one looks up at him and says something about an old house. I don't know what but his face just crumpled. Big Gordon: his face just crumpled.

I let go of her hand. Mr Popo was holding her and she was talking to him. She said 'Hello Mr Popo.' Her voice sounded funny, not like I had imagined. I don't remember everything she said. There was a joke and then Florence said something about his nose, which I thought was a bit rude. I didn't like that. I might have missed some of it because I wasn't listening properly. Miss Tench told Daddy I don't always listen properly. Then she was back with me, smiling as usual and not saying anything. They all clapped. That was the end.

It's over. I've done my bit. They didn't laugh much but they were probably just overawed, big occasion, that sort of thing. The look on that wee lassie's face when I did the ventriloquist bit, though. Pure astonishment. Made it all worthwhile, so it did.

When everyone had gone home I went out into the garden. It was cold but it wasn't raining. Florence smiled at me but she didn't say anything. I got the wee spade and dug a hole underneath the tree at the corner. Florence didn't fit at first so I had to make it a bit wider. I put half a brick on top of her before I filled it in. She still didn't say anything. Florence was my friend for such a long time and I told her

everything, everything there was to tell. Nobody else, just
Florence. All that time she never spoke to me. Why did she
have to talk to that man? She couldn't be my friend after
that. Traitor.

THE GARDEN-BOY

Sylvia Pearson

The air was murmurous with insects. Rianne stopped about five yards from a green msasa tree in her high-walled garden, set down the cooler box, and shook out a long velour towel on to a sun lounger already hot to the touch. This morning her mood, more elevated than it had been for several weeks, allowed her – but still in a detached way – to enjoy other sounds: the cool gurgling of doves in high oaks beyond her garden and behind that, in contrast, the metallic insistence of cicadas with their monotonous chirruping, an African chorus as relentless as time itself.

Time! Measured by the sun now almost directly overhead, no shadows to speak of except close against those walls from which came another sound, a man-made one, a rhythmic chip-chip as her garden-boy, Ezekiel, broke up sunbaked soil with a long-handled hoe. A shy boy this African, twenty, who travelled in every day from Soweto – recommended by her girl, Tembi.

'You can be safe with him, meddam; he is not one of thoz Young Lions who are causing all thoz troubles in Soweto, but truly it is becoming so hahd to find boys who would rathah carry a gahden spade than a knobkerrie or knives or a gun. Since Mandela was freed there is no peace in our township. Too many mothahs are afraid of their own sons – they do not know where they go and when they will come home with blood on their clothes!'

Rianne had needed to hear all this from Tembi. These were dangerous times. For a white woman such as she who had known the reassurance of being married to a Special

Branch policeman – well . . . she did not want to think about it. Six months in her employ now, she was satisfied with Ezekiel. He was reliable, respectful, never daring a direct gaze but with propriety, from lowered lids – as it should be. And monosyllabic – 'yes mem, no mem' in response to her orders. The only times she had seen him animated were in conversation with Tembi in her kitchen when a pot of tea was shared by the two, or when he asked permission to scrub his hands before eating a meagre packed lunch, taken seated in the cool interior of her garage.

Which was how Rianne had come to know the husky cadences of Ezekiel's voice, the clicks of his Xhosa speech, the space between his two front teeth, the cheap tiger's tooth necklace which jerked on the strings of his muscled neck as he chewed.

Today, Thursday, was Tembi's day off, but Rianne's needs had been anticipated. There were pan-fried curried-chicken drumsticks – complete with cutlet frills – and a lemon cheesecake in her fridge, mango sorbet in the freezer. But it was Tembi's cheerful, bustling presence in the house which Rianne missed. What did it matter about food? What need had she of sustenance now?

She felt her mood begin to spiral downwards and hastily unclipped the lid of the cooler box. Beer, Coca-Cola, fruit juice, white wine – which should she have? Wine would reach her more quickly. She drank deeply from a crystal glass of sparkling white, bubbles pricking the back of her throat, stabbing the heat-dried membranes of her nostrils.

Using the box as a table for her glass, she arranged herself on the lounger. A large sun brolly kept her upper body in shade. She shook out her long blonde hair, nudged expensive sunglasses back up on to the bridge of her nose and, after a final downward glance at her perfect figure in its black bikini, willed herself towards the mellowing effect of the wine.

From behind the safety of her dark goggles her eyes followed the lazy progress of the young African as he moved among the flower beds, stooping now and again to twitch out a weed, shaking it free of its red soil and throwing it behind him on to the grass. No sign that he was aware of her, but Rianne knew that Ezekiel had known the moment she had entered her garden. She could not greet him unless she required something of him. It simply was not done. And he could not speak until spoken to.

Later, she would take a swim in her pool, whose green waters would be warmer in an hour or so. Then he would be forced to some sign of acknowledgment – a hand to tip a nonexistent cap, the gleam of a tooth between full lips, a muttered 'meddam'. Her friends would be shocked at her flaunting her white body before a black. So what? Where were they, anyway, those friends? They rarely visited now. Avoiding her, unable to cope with her pain, her moods, her despair. If she needed their company she had to go to their houses by arrangement – an unspoken rule. Anger boiled up in her. The irony of it! Before her husband's death in that terrible Soweto riot theirs had been a full social life; parties, booze cruises on the Vaal river, bridge, sundowners, weekend barbeques in true Afrikaans tradition.

After Frank's death 'phone calls and invitations had dwindled. She had become that dangerous statistic – a woman without a man, receiving only occasional release from her prison by trusting female friends who knew her to be no maneater. And now, well . . . now, she was neither a threat nor a temptation.

Rianne flicked open the cooler box and sat up to refill her glass. The wine bottle clinked against a clutch of fruit juices. This brought Ezekiel up from his crouched position under a jacaranda. He half twisted and looked over his shoulder, turned away again. She saw him reach a hand up to wipe his brow and brush a purple feather of blossom from his thick rug of hair. She replaced the wine bottle, and drew forth a can of Castle beer, watching dribbles of condensation run down the golden tin.

'Baba!' she called, using the respectful term. 'Come, here's a beer for you – it's very hot today, hey.'

He stuck his trowel in the earth and, wiping his hands down the sides of baggy blue overalls unbuttoned to his waist, falteringly approached. She lay back languidly, the wine singing her mind to carelessness, holding the can of cold beer by her side.

'Mem?' She opened her eyes. He stood a yard away. She held up the can, beckoning with it. He took one more step, and stretched forth his hand, its palm stained with the red soil of her garden, his land. One fingertip touched hers briefly as he took the tin from her. It was cool against the warmth of hers.

'Thenk you, mem' – he held the tin against his body, just below his waist, and tugged the ringpull with a snap. The metal flashed in the sun as he raised it eagerly to his lips. Her eyes travelled slowly down from his bobbing Adam's apple, over his chest with its mat of coiled wires, and came to rest on that area below his waist allowed no definition by the looseness of his overalls. She tried to imagine, but couldn't because of the tug-of-war of revulsion and curiosity going on inside her. She drained her glass and sat up to recharge it once more, aware that she was exposing a deep cleavage as she leaned towards the box. Her ears were filled with the noise of his swallowing. She looked up in time to see his neat head swing down, and was shocked at his greed, at the speed with which he'd drunk the beer. He stood uncertain, juggling the empty can from hand to hand, his eyes flitting back and forth from her body to the beer tin. He grinned up at the sky – 'Thenks mem, that was very good.'

Rianne's head was swimming. She felt reckless. The next glass must be sipped slowly, very slowly. 'I suppose you would like another,' she said, the words out before she realized. The African stared out of wide, disbelieving eyes, their whites threaded with red from sun glare and dust and possibly the gulped beer.

'Mem?'

'Another beer, Ezekiel, you'd like another, hey? Thirsty work, gardening.'

He stood rooted to the spot, his lips trying to form words, hands clasped so tight round the can that blood suffused his pale fingernails and lightened his knuckles.

'Oh, for chrissake, man, sit down and help yourself – I'm going for a swim.' She stood up to face him, running a finger round the edges of her bikini, snapping the black Lycra against her thighs, adjusting her straps. Kicking off her sandals she swayed towards the pool. 'Oh, damn!' she said between her teeth, and returned for her swimming cap. A wry smile pulled at her mouth as she saw the African reach into the cooler box. His overalls swung forward, away from his spare frame, and she caught a glimpse of white briefs, his only garment beneath the thick blue cotton of his garden-boy uniform. Her tug-of-war rope broke and in its place a slow, fat worm uncoiled inside her, swelling, filling that part of her left empty, abandoned, deliberately ignored for two long years – and for the last few months, disowned, despised, dreaded!

Now it was Rianne's turn to lower her gaze, but too late – he had seen, had noticed, and the slow, careful change in his attitude was there on his face, in his body as he straightened, hooking a finger once more in the ringpull. Snap! He raised the can to his lips, arching his head, his back, with an exaggerated curve. And there it was, as the blue trousers flattened against his crotch, the definition for which she had searched earlier.

Staggering, Rianne made her way to the pool and dived into the shock of cold water. Four lengths of strong crawl she did and then, feeling the muzziness clear from her head, she turned on her back and floated, aware of the strong beat of her neck pulse below her chin. At the edge of her vision she could see him sprawled flat on his back, not beside her lounger, but in the shade of the green msasa tree on a white wrought-iron bench. His head to one side, he was watching her from under lowered lids. The fierce sun beat down on her and again that slow, fat worm coiled and uncoiled deep in her belly. And then she remembered. Her towel. She had not brought it to the pool's edge as she liked to do so that she could sit cloaked, with her feet in the shallows, letting the sun dry her without effort on her part.

'Ezekiel!' – her voice high and harsh. 'My towel, fetch my towel!'

His shadow fell over her just as she reached the tiled rim of the pool. She snatched off her rubber cap. Her golden swirl of thick hair fell around her shoulders. She hauled herself out of the water, and stepped over the scorched brick edge on to the lawn. He followed, hands awkwardly proffering the long Portuguese beach mat. She gestured impatiently for him to put it round her like a cape. His strong, peppery smell came to her with the yeasty odour of beer as he belched softly near her ear. She stopped and turned to face him, stroking herself dry through the luxury towel. He was smiling, a full, intimate smile. She could see the pink of his tongue through the space in his teeth.

'Bring the box into the house. Your stomach is rumbling like thunder. I'll give you some food. Leave your shoes outside.' No answer, but she heard the clatter of leather on stone and knew he followed close behind. Her mood! It was spiralling downwards again. Wine – she must have more wine. She pulled at random from the fridge chicken, ham, cheese, melon, a six-pack of Castle beer, and dumped it all on the kitchen table along with a bread box and Tembi's favourite knife.

Hitching herself up on to a high stool, she motioned for him to do the same. Taller than she by a head, he kept only one foot on the bar, resting the other on the floor, his toes splayed, leaving damp prints as they fidgeted like fingers. He ate voraciously, tearing flesh from chicken and ham bones, packing his cheeks till they bulged, cramming down bread and cheese, swallowing with grunts, the muscles of his jaws appearing and disappearing as he chewed. Disgusted by his manners, Rianne pushed some food around her plate, but drank steadily until the second bottle of the day stood empty.

Ezekiel stretched past her for the six-pack, and tore a can free. She was forced to watch the roll of his tongue as he cleared his teeth of food fragments, to listen to the suck and click of the pink muscle as it searched out and withdrew shreds of meat and bread. And then to see him gulp more beer, holding it in his cheeks like a mouthwash, a child's trick!

Rianne did not allow him to finish his drink. She pulled him up by the shoulder of his overalls. 'Get these off!' she demanded. 'You going to have a shower now.' He stared. 'Ja, you heard me, Kaffir, do it now!' He flinched at the sting of that word, and then slid off the stool, the beer still in his fist. 'Follow me,' she ordered, and heard the slow shuffle of his bare feet on the parquet floor leading to her bathroom. She slid the glass door of the cubicle open, switched on the preset spray of water, and stepped aside. 'Use *plenty* of soap, you hear, and there's a towel over there on a hook.'

Her voice was strong, controlled, but she was trembling inside. He was standing on one leg, pulling the other out of its blue trouser. His briefs were grey-white, bulging. She tried to look away, but couldn't. He drew his other leg out of his uniform and stamped on it. She left him in her ensuite bathroom, walked away from the bundle on the floor with its smudges of red soil, its rank smell of his sweat, his discarded briefs which still held the shape of him.

She drew her bedroom curtains against the glare of sun, peeled off her bikini, and lay on the white satin bedspread. And waited – pushing aside all thoughts except those dictated by that rearing monster in her belly. Why shouldn't she? Why not – after all this time of loneliness after Frank's death, and then the other . . . the other! She deserved something out of all this, surely. Her anger surfaced, strengthened her resolve.

She heard the rasp of the shower door, but the noise of the shower went on, its jets of water drumming walls and floor. Of course! He did not know how to switch it off, her African garden-boy. Typical!

He came to her in a cloud of her husband's Paco Rabane never before removed from its shelf – not dried, some foam still flecking his hair and chest, splayed fingers dashing water from his eyes, pinching his nostrils clear in his African way. The mattress dipped as he sat on the edge of her bed, looking down at her, smiling.

'You have not dried yourself, boy!'

His smile vanished. He leapt on to the bed, kneeling astride her so that his swollen phallus swayed close to her face like a black mamba poised to strike. He laid his whole length on top of her. The cheap tiger's-tooth necklace dripped water into her eyes.

'Wait!' she gasped. 'Wait – you must first put this on!' she ordered. And then a sudden rush of concern swept through her. Needles of anxiety pricked the veins in her throat, and she was overcome by the primitive fear of his blackness.

The African youth squinted down at the condom which she was pressing against his chest. His face twisted with scorn. 'We African men *nevah* use such things.' He laughed, throwing back his head, and she could see the high vault of his mouth. He snatched the piece of latex from her fingers and flicked it far across the room.

This time she begged, twisting her head away from him, straining an arm towards the open bedside drawer. 'Please,' she gasped. 'Let me – put – one on for you – it is better – you won't even notice . . .' but he was kneeing her legs apart now and pinning her arms down with his.

'Hah!' he snorted. He took her savagely, swiftly, without thought for her pleasure or comfort. Heavy on her, she had to snatch breaths when she could. It was over in minutes, his breath tearing out of him in long, ragged wheezes. He relaxed, remained inside her for a long time. At last, realizing that he had fallen asleep, she eased first one leg and then the other from under him and, rolling on to her side with her back to him, curled up, sobbing noisily.

She lay in the foetal position for some time and then her skin began to cool and contract, and she shivered. The drumming of the shower. She must wash now. But could she wash away the foulness of this act? Could she? And the guilt – what of that? But the guilt was not entirely hers. And had she not *begged* him to use the condom? Of course she had. But those macho African men! She could not be held responsible for their stupid ways. It would not be *her* fault if he contracted her disease. And in any case, had it not originated here, in Africa, *his* country?

FISH OUT OF WATER

Lynne Bryan

Monday morning Christopher phones. Christopher with his lanky body, his Roman nose. Christopher with his guilt. Ellie listens to his polite voice, the apologies which are supposed to make her feel better, the offer of money, the gift of the flat. She listens, then replaces the receiver. Quick. Before she tells him about the dark line their baby has drawn on the hump of her belly. Before she showers him with the intimacy he no longer wants. The intimacy she needs to forget.

Monday afternoon Ellie bags Christopher's belongings and leaves them on the landing outside their flat. She hoovers the carpets, cleans every surface, empties the waste-paper baskets which still hold paper scraps covered in his neat chilly writing. Then she tries to squeeze a king-size quilt into her washing machine, wanting to wash away the remnants: the smells of massage oil and sex, his naked smell. But the quilt will not fit.

Ellie will have to brave the laundrette. But it is Wednesday before she does. She has never used the laundrette, nor any of the other businesses at the end of her street. She has felt too much of an outsider, with her accent, her looks. She is not from this area.

The laundrette is crammed between the post office and the public toilets. It is an old building. Shabby. Despite the bright blue woodwork, the artfully painted sign, and the Fablon fishes which swim across the display window.

The owner of the laundrette is called John. Everybody

calls him John. Nobody knows his surname. The hand-painted sign above the laundrette door reads, PERSONAL SERVICE LAUNDRETTE. PROPRIETOR – JOHN.

John wears a deep crimson suit in winter, orange shorts in summer. He has a lot of hats. Each day he parades the length of his laundrette, twirling like a model, showing off his clothes. The men who work at the local shipyards, with their oil-streaked skin, make a mockery of John. But others appreciate his campness, his bigger than bigness. John is their crazy man. The golden fry in their grey-fry lives.

The laundrette is narrow and cluttered. Washing machines line one wall, chairs and a spin dryer the other, while at the back stands a row of ancient de luxe dryers. These dryers are buttermilk yellow, taller than a human, and look condemned. Fishes decorate most of the machines and a border of blue paint divides the concrete floor from the Artex walls.

Ellie walks to the laundrette. She feels conspicuous. Too bright for the grey buildings, the passers-by dressed in shades of brown and beige. A shabby patch. Christopher's choice because the flat was cheap and big, and besides Christopher had a car which meant he wasn't tied to the shabbiness. He could escape.

Ellie had met Christopher at work. He'd sat next to her in the canteen, causing her hands to shake nervously as she had forked her chips. She had been flattered when he'd asked her to minute meetings for him, to move offices and cities with him, to share his life. Now, she does not know what she expected. Only she never expected his sudden resentment, his dissatisfaction. She never expected him to transfer home without her.

Ellie edges into the laundrette. She sniffs the smell of damp and standing water, registers its threadbareness, the row of customers sitting on blue plastic chairs facing the washing machines. They are local-looking, sallow-skinned. But they acknowledge Ellie, make her feel welcome. Particularly the elderly women. 'Come in. Come in,' they both greet.

Ellie looks at the women, wonders whether they are related. The way they speak together, heads dressed with the same short hairstyle. She notes their iron-flat bottoms and matching Crimplene trousers. One rises from her chair to transfer her washing from the washing machine to the spinner. The grey-looking garments drip on the concrete floor. The other pats the empty chair next to her, inviting Ellie to sit.

'Thank you,' says Ellie, easing onto the chair. She places her hands under her bump, lifting the weight off her bladder.

'John'll be out in a minute,' says the woman, lighting a fag. She waves it at Ellie. 'I hope you don't mind,' she says. 'But I'm terribly addicted.'

'It's OK,' says Ellie, not wishing to offend. 'I understand.'

A toilet flushes. Ellie turns towards the sound and spies a thin spout of a man. Dressed in orange shorts, scarlet shirt and green pork pie hat.

Ellie almost whistles. Like Christopher used to whistle at things strange or beautiful. An amazed whistle. A congratulatory whistle. A whistle sometimes directed at her when she wore her evening dress with the scalloped hem. The dress which made her shimmer and froth at Christopher's business meals. The dress which she hid beneath her coat as she stepped from the flat to Christopher's car.

John sashays towards her. His hands outstretched, his face covered with ginger-red pan-stick. 'And what can I do for you?' he smiles.

Ellie holds out her bag. John up-ends it, shaking the linen on to the floor. 'Lovely,' he says. 'My speciality.'

'Oh,' says Ellie. She looks from John to her quilt. She maps the creamy stains, smells the intimate bedtime smell, and blushes. 'It's ages old,' she defends. 'I'm afraid I . . .'

John places a finger on his lips: a finger decorated with

a coral ring. Shush, he mouths. Then, gently, he lifts the quilt to coax it into the drum of a washing machine.

'Thank you,' says Ellie, grateful for his discretion. 'Thank you very much.'

John raises his hat. 'No problem,' he says. He bends to switch on the machine, the seat of his shorts stretching to frame his slim backside. Then he turns to whisper in her ear. 'If you need the toilet,' he says, 'it's out the back.'

'Oh,' says Ellie. 'Well, yes.'

'Right, follow me,' John says. He raises a latch on a rough tongue-and-groove door and opens it. Wide. 'Plenty of space,' he says.

Ellie manoeuvres past John and through the doorway. She is conscious of her navel, pushed out by the developing foetus, poking beneath her T-shirt. It brushes against John. And she flusters. She is happy to be pregnant, but also ashamed. She is ashamed of how her body has grown, how awkwardly it advertises what she wants to keep private.

She remembers having a fight with Christopher over her size. 'I'll soon be able to drown in your flesh,' he teased, pushing his face down between her breasts. A mock fight. An affectionate fight.

Ellie perches on the toilet. She runs her hands over her belly, sees the baby swim beneath her skin. Only last week she and Christopher were at the hospital, discussing his role, how he should be there when the waters break, to mop her brow, to cut the cord, to cry with her. And now?

Ellie pulls the flush, watches the greeny jet of water shoot around the dirty pan. Through the sound she can hear John, teasing his customers. Ellie smiles. Pleased to have found this place.

She leaves the toilet to find John seated at a tatty card table. The table is piled with mail, a silver-coloured cash box, and a newspaper. The newspaper is folded, with the quick crossword showing. John lifts a pen from a small leather pouch strung around his waist, and taps it on the crossword.

The woman with the fag invites Ellie to sit again. She leans towards Ellie, cigarette ash dressing her chin. 'This is fun,' she confides.

'Now . . .' says John. He stretches his arms, links his fingers together, pushing till they crack. 'What's got eight letters, begins with "S" and means to pl . . . unge?' John dips his hands deep beneath the table. 'Or to s . . . ink?' John nips his nose between his fingers, makes glug glug noises like an emptying drain.

A man nearing eighty shuffles to look at the crossword. He wears a full three-piece suit and a kipper tie. He has no teeth, and seems unable to form proper words. John winks at him, 'Not you, Joe,' he says. 'You just concentrate on your smalls. I'm wanting an answer from the smart girls. Margaret? Mary?'

The two elderly women shake their heads. 'No idea, John,' they say.

'How about you, then?' asks John, looking at a boy.

The boy lowers his eyes, moves to watch his football kit and track pants flick their desultory way around the innards of a de luxe dryer. The dryer slows and the boy clicks open the door to pull out the load. John walks over to help him. He takes the washing from the boy's arms and stuffs it in a bin-bag. 'Submerge,' he says to the boy. 'The word I'm looking for is submerge. I submerge. You submerge. We all submerge.'

The boy says, 'Oh.' He slips a hand into his trouser pocket, removes some change. John watches over the boy as he fumbles to select the right coins.

'Here let me,' John says. He takes the boy's hand, spreading the slight palm flat with his ringed fingers. 'Just like choosing chocolates,' he winks. He lifts the coins. One by one. Fake kissing the Queen's head before dropping them, chinking, into his leather pouch.

'Don't be wicked, John,' laughs the elderly woman with the fag. 'You'll embarrass the boy.' Smoke rushes from her mouth and Ellie shifts heavily in her chair, turning her head from the smell.

John ushers the boy from the laundrette, then wanders over to look at Ellie's washer. 'The red light is out,' he says. Ellie grips the plastic chair and tries to push herself up. 'No, don't.' John flags her to sit. 'I'll put it in the dryer. We can't have you straining yourself.'

John pulls the quilt from the washer. Ellie notices that the quilt is not whiter than white, that some stains remain. John lifts the quilt, holds it to the light. 'Not bad,' he comments. 'Not as bad as old Mac's. Remember that, ladies? He swore it was just dirt. I told him just dirt wouldn't stick to the fabric like that. Just dirt would disappear.' John bundles the quilt into a de luxe dryer, and slams shut the glass-dome door.

'Ah, but he's a weird one,' remarks the elderly woman with the fag. She moves the fag like she is underlining words on a blackboard, a teacher making a point.

Ellie closes her eyes and bathes in the sound of John and his customers. She hasn't heard much chat since Christopher left, since his call. Only chat on the television, and her neighbours' voices. Muffled voices coming through the thin wall behind her bookcase. Voices which belong to the young couple who ignore her, who ran coins down the side of Christopher's car.

The woman with the clothes in the spinner removes them. She holds each item against her face to test for dampness, before stuffing it in her basket on wheels. 'Well,' she says. 'That's me.'

'And that's £2.50,' says John.

The woman nods and opens her plastic purse. She fumbles around. 'More bus tickets than money,' she sighs.

The elderly man laughs. 'Shut it, you,' says John. 'Or you're banned.'

'Don't ban,' begs the elderly man. 'Don't ban.' He

looks down at his kipper tie, touches its flowery point.

'Bless him,' says the woman with the fag.

'Oh, don't be conned,' says John. He places an arm round the elderly man's shoulders. The man smiles at John, and makes loving noises. 'This guy is fly. He gets tea and biscuits from me every day, and not once has he paid for his washing.'

'Perhaps I should play potty,' says the woman. 'Get my stuff done for free.'

'And do me out of business,' John winks. 'You'd miss me, Mary. I'm the only man in your life.'

'Some man,' laughs the woman. She edges towards John, puckering her lips.

Ellie is the last to leave the laundrette. Her quilt has taken a long while to dry in the de luxe dryer. John apologizes, but she says it doesn't matter, that she has enjoyed her morning. 'I was feeling a little sad,' she says. 'You've cheered me up.'

'Glad to hear it,' smiles John. 'I do my best.' He gestures at the machinery, now standing idle on the bare concrete floor, the plastic measuring cups empty of soap powder, the tatty price list peeling from the wall. 'It's difficult, but . . .' he smiles again.

'Yes,' says Ellie. 'It is.' She pays John, and carries her quilt from the laundrette. John bolts the laundrette door behind her, turning his OPEN sign to WE ALL NEED LUNCH BREAKS.

Alone on the street Ellie feels a chill. A cool breeze carrying the stench of the nearby sewerage works, the sounds of mothers chastising their kids, those distinctive guttural voices that Christopher used to mimic. Ellie glances back to the warmth of the laundrette, wanting to quell the rush of memories, the bleak lonely feeling she almost forgot while guessing crossword clues, watching John parade his costume, tilting his pork pie at enticing angles. She squints through the murky glass, hoping to reassure herself. A last glimpse of someone as alien as her, yet managing. Like a fish out of water, turned amphibious.

When Ellie arrives at her flat she unbundles her quilt, lays it on the bed. She smells the sweet smell of cheap soap powder, traces the mottled pattern of diminished stains. She climbs beneath the quilt, piles pillows under her belly, and curls to rest.

She closes her eyes, and recalls John as she saw him through the laundrette window. He was leaning into a de luxe dryer, wiping a rag around the drum. A dull shift covering his bright bright clothes. The shift which made her shiver and fear for herself. Until John turned round to acknowledge her tapping upon the window. His smile golden, joyous, unchanged.

At least that was how Ellie saw the smile. Needing to ignore the brief moment before when John looked different. His face as chilly and grey as the concrete floor of his laundrette. His slight form swamped by the ageing machinery, mocked by the flicking tails of his Fablon fishes.

A DOG'S LIFE

Alan Warner

It was too beautiful an evening to be thinking about killing the dog.

The homesick old man watched birds going inland, black against the luminosity of the Mediterranean twilight, and he licked his lips. For ten years of retirement the old man and his wife had lived in the resort and the initial, terrible homesickness had never left him. As the sky turned a hue of peach in towards the vicious arêtes of Ondara he thought of home: green hills with blisters of darker heather and mists blowing across them.

Meanwhile the glossy boxer dog trotted on ahead, poking his snout into the dry scrub sprouting over the broken kerb underneath the pines. The old man didn't let the dog venture far out of sight. Hunters put down fox poison on these hills and his wife loved the dog fanatically.

Around the sleek villas on the pine hills the sounds of construction had gone on all afternoon. Among the avenues it was now very quiet except for the distant buzz of the odd scooter motoring down to the sea. One day the avenues would be lined with holiday villas and telegraph wires. There were no villas at that moment although each avenue had a new nameplate.

The old man shouted the dog's name and it followed him up the steep avenue beyond the unconnected electricity terminals. By a particular aluminium box where the scrub was sparse the man stepped over the kerb and into the pines. The rough tree trunks were not close together. There was a plastic bag by some roots with a broken breeze block on top of it. The old man stooped and grunted as he removed the breeze block. The dog stood on the kerb watching and wagging its docked tail curiously for a few seconds, then snorting, it sniffed on down the kerb. The man took out the half-full bottle of Gordons, unscrewed the cap which scratched a little as if grit was under it and drank. The glow of that evening seemed to be trapped in the brilliant liquid which always looked thicker than water to him.

He replaced the bottle and the breeze block then, calling the dog's name, he left the trees. The dog came panting, ears back and the old man clipped the leash to its collar. The dog tugged him down the deserted avenues to the parked car. Perfect stars pushed out the smooth sky.

The small villa sat off the road beyond the more ostentatious turrets of the Swiss and German neighbours. The bungalow-style villa was in a stretch of garden, fenced in for the dog. Even in the dark, marigolds and calendulas were bright.

The scullery windows were steamed up and the old woman was boiling tatties and Brussels sprouts.

'A chill out now, Mother.'

'Hello, little fellow,' she said, bending slowly down to the dog. 'Just you have a little brown bread and honey piece while I do Daddy's silly potatoes.'

'A chill out, Mother.'

'Aye. I heard you. It's a south-westerly, always brings the cold.'

The old woman was always declaring that a particular wind direction was responsible for the weather. While it wasn't a pretension, just a habit, it irritated him because he was certain her meteorology was unsound.

When the tatties had boiled enough she drained them and abandoned the meal to cut up lean bits of chicken for the dog. The old woman had long ago retreated into that easy refuge: hatred of people and love of animals.

The old man put on some long slacks and lit the gas fire

that wheeled about When he went to pull the curtains the last light of the sunset silhouetted the gargantuan mountain of the Mongo; behind the village it looked like a mammoth battleship moving across the black earth.

He had to wait until the dog had finished eating before she reheated the tatties and sprouts and took the chops from the grill. She only put veg on her plate as they both sat at the scullery table with the boxer dog curled up by the cooker. They didn't talk and the old man had the radio placed on the table, with the sober voices of the World Service intoning loudly.

After eating he washed the pots and dishes while his wife sat in their room by the gas heater watching the telly, with a dictionary on the armrest. The boxer lay at her feet on a rug to keep him off the stone floor. If a word was said on the programme which she didn't understand she turned the pages of the dictionary, talking to the dog about it. With its pink tongue the boxer dog licked off a sticking plaster from her shin then spat out the flesh-coloured plastic.

The old man went straight to bed so he could rise early when most of his drinking would be done. He dozed in the bed reading bits of a Desmond Bagley novel from the English language library in the village. He dropped the book twice as he nodded off and drank from the bottle of brandy hidden high up in the wardrobe.

Hours later the old lady put the dog to bed under blankets on the couch and went to a room where she slept alone.

He got up soon after first light and went out to the garden where he had hidden in a bush, a bottle of Gordons. In the bright early light coming across the bushes and dusted with busy insects he poured out a full glass and replaced the bottle. He took the glass into the scullery and transferred half of it into another glass that he hid in a high-up cupboard, beyond the reach of the old woman. He refilled the glass with some tap water and took a long swig. He turned up the World Service and began to fry bacon. He used bread to wipe his plate clear of egg yolk then, after washing the dishes, he squeezed some oranges into a glass. He took the glass into his wife's room.

'Wake up, Mother,' he said.

Before she came from her bedroom he drank the other glass of gin and washed it.

In the morning the sun was still cool so they pottered in the garden and the dog watched them as it lay in the shade cast by the bungalow.

In the afternoon the old couple sat in the sun for a little while. Both their bodies were prone in the light battering down on the terrace, the man sweating. Pinioned in that glare his body seemed to go numb as thought became dominant. He thought of cold, real winter where bitter mornings numb your nose as if it was pinched between finger and thumb. He thought of the mountains when he was young, after the war. In the evening all the friends from the mess hall and their girlies would requisition the town fire-tender and load it with beer. He remembered the girls' stockings showing as they climbed up into the machine. Bottles popped as the fire-tender curved up the sides of the mountain to the banks of the frozen lake. As the sun sank they sprayed a huge arc of water over the ice with the fire hose. As the temperature fell with the sun going down over the ridge, the pools on the ice froze into a perfect skating surface. They swung the great searchlight across the ice, lighting up the mountain face on the other side of the lake then laced their skates on and cut in and out of the darkness, racing each other in circles.

The old lady was also thinking. She remembered the summer pool by the hired cottage. The heatwave night that six of them, all teenagers from the next crofts, pinched the bottle of rum from the big house. Drunk, they sneaked to the river, boys and girls stripping in the total blackness of the night. Silently, the six of them slipped into the dark water. There was no moon, she only saw the whiteness of the body next to her when it was as close as you could get. Cautiously, she swam beside one of the boys.

Suddenly Strachan's police car materialized up on the bridge. The headlights came bracing across the surface of the pool. Next to her the face that was illuminated in the beam of light was a strange one, a boy she had never seen before. She screamed and other screams came from across the pool, more than six voices: a group of teenagers had *already* been silently swimming in the illicit, dark pool when her group had climbed in. Young fingers had reached towards bodies they believed they knew in the dark until Strachan's headlights strayed onto and held the scene. Young naked bodies pranced clear of the water in a frantic search for clothes and to escape the light. Some made for the hired cottage, others crouched in the shadows and trees round the pool. When the screams died down Strachan's laughter up by the bridge was the only sound.

The old man stood up. Moving around inside the villa, his head seemed full of a blue buzzing.

The old lady came in.

'Mother, I want us to sell up and go back home.'

'If I've told you once, you know we can't go with the dog. The wee boy is too old to survive that flight home and six months in quarantine. Put on a shirt, you'll get the chill. Look at you, you're stinking with sweat.'

'Mother, I know why I want to go home. It's nothing to do with silly nostalgia. I don't want to die in this country and be in the ground within twenty-four hours.'

'Fiddlesticks, man. You're not going to die yet. All that booze in you has pickled you. It's me that'll die, pulling my guts out looking after you day in day out. Or you'll take a stroke and I'll be left *here*, wiping your arse for you more than I do now. Besides, you have to stay here, it'll take a year to sell this cattleshed. You were too lazy to look after the last garden and now you can't be bothered with this one. Just 'cause you take the wee boy for a walk you think you're absolved, well, by christ that'll be right. Your attitude has always just been that there are two things in this country: dust and cheap liquor. You've always had that weak streak in you . . .'

With his wife still talking, the old man walked out to the bush and drank straight from the hot gin bottle in the broad daylight.

As the heat lifted that afternoon he drove up to the undeveloped pine hills to give the dog its daily walk. He went directly to the bottle among the trees and gulped more than usual.

At a hollow where the ground was scattered with shotgun cartridges from the Sunday hunters a bit of dried meat rested on a rock, circled by ant repellent: strychnine for foxes. The old man placed it in a bit of newspaper and went home.

He secretly fed the meat to the dog the next morning. Soon it lay panting on the stone floor looking as if its heart would burst. The old lady wailed in pity, rocking forwards and backwards holding the dog. Sometimes she asked what was wrong, sometimes she moaned the dog or her husband's name. By the time he came back with the vet, paroxysms were wracking the animal every few minutes; brown liquid and wind spat from under its tail as the back legs stiffened and its body revolted against the poison. The old man was shocked the vet would not put the dog down. The old man took him through to the scullery then tried to give him money, but the vet wouldn't kill the dog. The three of them watched.

Towards night a final convulsion locked the hindlegs, its eyes became distant and the dog died. His wife would not leave the side of the warm animal and long slivers of saliva and snotter dropped from her face onto the dead dog.

Outside the old man paid the vet in the darkness then, as the van left, he drank from the bottle.

Back in the room he said, 'Oh Mother, why do things have to be so sad?'

She said his name, then she said, 'Things would be less sad if men didn't do truly wicked things.'

'What do you mean?'

She began to cry and though he should have comforted her he went to bed and she cried alone.

The next day, before the heat was too much, he sweated, digging a deep hole in among the marigolds and calendulas. The corpse had already begun to smell as its innards decomposed.

She struggled to wrap the dog in its blankets and they put it in the hole with its toys. The old man layered stones on top of the blankets then shovelled in soil.

'I'm leaving you. I hate you,' she said. 'The wee fellow kept us together but there's nothing now. I've booked the flight. You can go about selling this cattleshed and we'll split what's left.'

'Don't go,' he said.

She went back among the hills and mists he only dreamed of. He had to try and sell the house in winter. He drank too much from the bottles on the tables. He didn't like to go out where the grave was. He hired a cleaner but soon told her just to leave the shopping and gin at the gate. He never got the correct change but he couldn't argue in their language. He stopped cleaning the rooms and hanging out washing. A man alone, he ate his food straight from the greasy frying pan.

One night his wife telephoned. He was drunk and couldn't follow each word. She spoke of their investments and her solicitor. Her voice echoed and then he just hung up.

*　　*　　*

It was a winter night, as if all the good in the world was rising up like hot air to the cold stars and leaving only wickedness on the planet. The old man sat in a dark room. His red face blazed, his nose looked blue and his eyes watery.

JUVENILE

Ruth Thomas

Mary is in the kitchen, filling up the ice bucket. She has been working for a minute or so, beginning almost to enjoy herself, when she sees Mr Sullivan's size fourteen shoes come squashing down the steps. At knee-height is a large bunch of orange chrysanthemums. The shoes and flowers turn a precise forty-five degrees. Then she hears him saying something to his daughters in the garden. His voice is loud, rising higher, but theirs are sad when they wail back across the flowerbeds. After a while, Mr Sullivan opens the kitchen door and thuds past the table, rattling the ice cubes.

'Can you make sure they don't scrape chalk all over the garden, Mary?' he says. 'I've got people coming round this afternoon.' Then he goes upstairs with the chrysanthemums to find his wife. It is a strange relationship: distant and unformed, though still with traditions in it of affection, like flowers and cool kisses.

But the house is hot. Even in the summer, Mrs Sullivan makes sure the heating stays on, so that it resembles a palace in Rangoon – humid and heavy – and Mary has to run about with the ice. There is an intercom between the kitchen and the living room, where Mrs Sullivan watches videos. When she gets bored, she summons Mary for drinks or some piece of food – two unbuttered crackers or a bowl of yoghurt. But most of the time Mary stays in the basement, below railings and people's feet. When she looks up, there are sometimes people peering down at her, as if she is in a doll's house. She gives them the thumbs-up, which disconcerts them and makes her laugh.

She made up her CV because Mrs Sullivan would not have taken her without qualifications – although she has cooked and cleaned without them for forty years. And the payment she receives sounds generous, but not when she takes into account the hours she works. In the mornings she arrives early and heads for the kitchen, picking up the post on the way, putting on her apron, clicking the kettle for tea. Then she does kippers or porridge. And every time one of the family has a bath, she has to clean the bathroom, replacing towels on the rail, poking round the taps, pulling hairs off the soap. And in the afternoons she has to iron huge shirts, because Mr Sullivan attends a lot of meetings. His daughters' clothes are tiny in comparison. When Mary irons their vests and knickers she is always shocked at the difference. Size six Mickey Mouse versus XL Van Heusen.

By the end of the week, her mind is like the house – full of debris and difficult corners. 'You can take Sunday afternoons off,' Mrs Sullivan said when she gave her the job. 'I expect you like to attend church.' But Mary does not like to attend church. She goes for long walks in the park to air her head.

This Sunday Mrs Sullivan has asked her to do roast beef plus things she calls 'trimmings'. She is not sure about pudding so she slinks silkily into the living room with a recipe book, and a few minutes later her voice sighs across the intercom, 'Crème caramel please, Mary.' Then she switches on her new work-out video. Mary hears music through the kitchen ceiling.

As Mrs Sullivan has not bothered to return the recipe book, she hunts for another in the kitchen drawer and finds the recipe:

> 4 eggs
> 1 pt milk
> Vanilla essence
> 1–2 oz sugar

The custard ingredients are simple enough, and the caramel is basically sugar and water, heated gently.

'Grease the dariole moulds,' begins the recipe. She has never seen or heard of a dariole mould before, but finds some little dishes in the cupboard and smears butter inside them. Then she crouches at the fridge, and climbs onto a chair at the cupboard, for sugar, eggs, milk, vanilla.

'Place sugar in a thick pan and add water and lemon juice.' Mary is efficient at cooking: she does what the recipe tells her, to avoid mistakes. This one says that she should heat the sugar very slowly. After a while the crystals dissolve and she turns the heat up, stirring until the liquid turns brown and smells thick and sweet, like molasses.

Upstairs, Mrs Sullivan has turned the video down and Mary can hear her voice proclaiming loud pleasure about the flowers. She even hears a cool kiss. Then the video is turned up again and she hears the big shoes walking out of the room. For a while, Mr Sullivan throws his weight about clumsily in the drawing room; alone, not knowing where to go. Mary imagines him flicking through a magazine or staring out of the window, big and futile. This house is sad; nothing but centrally-heated emptiness. And mealtimes are as silent as leaves falling; Mary listens to it as she washes up in the kitchen. It used to annoy her that no-one thanked her for the meals, because they obviously enjoy them. The plates are always spotless. But she has realized that enjoyment embarrasses them. The daughters are being warned against it. So these days she just feels sorry for them.

Mary takes the pan off the heat and pours caramel into the dishes. It looks just like the photographs on caramel mix packets and, pouring the custard on top, she wonders if it was worth the effort. But the beef is beginning to smell good, and spitting fierce explosions. She opens the oven door and chucks potatoes in the tray. One good thing about working for the Sullivans is that she eats well, even if she is alone. She looks forward to eating these meals. The ingredients are always the best.

'To test custard, insert a pointed knife into the base of

one mould. Cool in a refrigerator.' Now that everything is doing what it should, cooling in the fridge or roasting in the oven, she has time to set the table. She gets out a dented metal tray and puts cutlery and napkins on it. She always used to forget the jug of iced water but now she puts it on first, to avoid complaints. The ice makes a beautiful sound. It makes her realize how hot she is. Her feet are damp inside her shoes.

'Mary, can you come out for a minute, please?'

The oldest daughter is standing on the kitchen doorstep, hard and small and nervy. She looks ashamed, as if she should not need to talk to Mary. But there is something she requires. The hopscotch finished a while ago. They have finished scratching chalk on the path, squashing stray bits of lavender beneath their sandals.

Since Mary started working there, she has seen the oldest girl freeze like Snow White, as if she needs the central heating to warm her up. She wears her mother's gold jewellery and mocks her sister with her mother's words. But the youngest daughter is still soft at the edges. She still plays games, stands in the kitchen watching Mary cook, recites things from joke collections. Mary puts down the tray and goes into the garden. Cool air runs at her down the steps. In front of her, Snow White is walking impatiently in her sandals, bangles and buckles ringing. Then she stops at the top of the path as if she has hit a wall, and points.

Underneath a big star-flowered bush lies a cat with a blackbird in its mouth. Squashing songs out, as if it is playing the harmonica, its teeth in the bird's neck. It makes Mary think of wildlife programmes, of cheetahs and antelope. She stares. The cat stares. The cat's grip is glum but determined, choking the bird, choking it, but the bird is still alive, making a strange sound like water running off a stone. It is the sound that makes Mary suddenly furious. She feels her skin heat and she swears up the steps, maddening her face, snagging her tights on an iron bannister. Her arms are already whirling about in the air and she screams at the cat, not even aware what she is saying. The cat drops the bird quickly and slinks into the neighbour's garden with its mouth open.

'Will it be all right?' says the smallest girl. She crouches on the path with a piece of chalk in her hand. The bird's new feathers have been ripped out and the bald patch on its head makes it look like a tiny human. There is no blood but Mary sees it flowing pink under the skin.

'Poor bird,' Mary says. Cats have such a cruel way of killing things.

'Will it be all right?' repeats the girl. 'What will you do with it?'

'I'll put it in a box and take it to the park after lunch.'

'Can I come with you?'

'Don't be juvenile,' says her sister, using their mother's word. 'We've got to go shopping this afternoon.'

When Mary looks at the youngest girl, her face is hot as if she has been slapped. She looks unsure where to go, scratching a triangle of chalk with her thumb against the path. Mary sighs and goes indoors to look for a box.

The dining room is sticky even though Mary had left the curtains closed to stop the sun getting in. When she draws them, she sees little wisps of dust in the light. She sets the table. Mr Sullivan has placed his chrysanthemums in the middle with uncharacteristic panache.

Retreating to the kitchen, Mary returns with lunch, carrying three plates at a time. She does her serving performance – lobs broccoli florets and roast potatoes onto the family's plates, pours wine for the parents and juice for the children. Mr Sullivan has eased his weight into the biggest chair and is reprimanding the youngest girl again for scraping chalk on the terrace. The girl just looks at the gravy jug and says nothing. She does not talk about the bird. She is learning that it is best not to talk.

On Sundays, Mary still finds it difficult to believe the scene in the dining room: the distracted chewing of the parents, the loose-mouthed boredom of the children. All eyes are focused on some point in the middle of the table. The chrysanthemums look stupidly jolly. She shuts the door and leaves them to it. In the kitchen, while the family eats, she carves herself some beef and puts it in a plastic bag to take home. She will layer it in sandwiches with mustard – her favourite way to eat roast beef, never mind the Yorkshire puddings and roast potatoes. Then she goes to look at the bird, which she has put in a Famous Grouse box in the ironing room. She was pleased to find the box and let the bird recover in it, incognito, for a while. It still sits in the corner, staring with black eyes, opening its yellow mouth without making any sound. Mary is touched by its determination. Its wings are folded properly now, but the head still sways, fragile as a nut, full of fearful bird-thoughts.

When lunch is over the family disappears, tired with heat and food, to separate rooms. Mary washes up. She notices that Mrs Sullivan has mushed her crème caramel into a wobbly mess and she swears. She always ends up swearing on a Sunday. As usual, everything else has been wolfed down. These dishes are always the worst because of the gravy but she also washes them quickest on Sundays because she does not want to lose her afternoon.

Before she is intercommed to do anything else, she wipes the table and draining board, takes off her apron, brushes her hair and collects the bird. Now it is more lively and seems to be studying the words on the side-flap. BY APPOINTMENT TO HER MAJESTY THE QUEEN. FINEST SCOTCH WHISKY. And it does accept the box regally, as if it is a carriage.

Outside, the Sullivans' car is standing half on the pavement, with the engine running. And both the girls are perched in it, waiting to go Sunday shopping with their mother. They do not talk; they stare out of opposite windows. But the youngest notices Mary with the box and gives her the thumbs-up. She has picked up her habit, and it is so out of place that it makes Mary laugh. And she laughs because the heat of the house always falls off her like a blanket when she shuts the kitchen door. She pretends for a while that she will never have to go back. And when she gets to the park she just sits on the grass and airs her mind. There is no point being unhappy; it is a waste of time. She just lets the bird go and closes her eyes.

NAVIGATOR

Duncan McLean

The Cutty Sark shut at three and we moved on.

Once I've paid up my house, I said, You'll not catch me offshore. I'll jack that in and never go near the fucking sea.

It wouldn't be so bad if you could move around a bit, said Finn. Follow the fucking sun, ken. It's just being stuck in the one place that's the bastard.

I started to cross the road, then walked on. Ach, it's just the seaman's mission. I thought it was a bar.

I'm going to get myself a boat, said Finn. One with a bed and a wee cooker and everything. That's the fucking ticket. Then head off into the wild blue yonder: point the nose of the thing for the equator and cheerio!

Where the fuck's that pub from last time? I said. What's it called? The Schooner . . .

Finn pushed open a shop door. Quick, in here . . .

I followed him. There were ropes and buoys on the floor, lifejackets and flares and compasses on shelves, and maps of the sea on the walls.

I want some of those, said Finn.

Charts? said the guy behind the counter.

Aye.

Where of?

The Sargasso Sea, said Finn. Zanzibar, North-west Iceland, Honolulu, the Great Barrier Reef, Van Diemen's Land, the Amazon Basin, Timbuktu, Montego Bay . . .

We only stock British coastal charts, said the guy.

What!

The guy shrugged. Sorry.

Shit . . . Finn leant his hands on the counter, his head hanging down. He seemed to be away to burst out greeting.

I gave him a clap on the shoulder. Never mind, I said, then turned to the shopkeeper. Could you tell us how to get to The Schooner Bar? I said.

FLAGS OF CONVENIENCE

Andrew Greig

That winter the front door scraped then clunked however cannily it was opened. He was awake in the dark and the gale sounded louder than before. His bedroom door clicked and there was a darker darkness beside it. He knew who it was because it couldn't be.

'Are you awake?' she whispered. 'Sorry.'

'Call by anytime,' he said. He was entirely calm. Like the bad news on the radio, it couldn't happen, it has happened, of course it had to happen.

'Sorry,' she said again. She sounded hoarse.

'What time is it?'

The darkness detached itself from the door, drifted further into the room.

'I won't stay, Malcolm,' she said. 'I've been at a party and it was too much and I'm just sheltering a moment to avoid someone.'

A gust hit like a fist on the big window. There was a clatter in the alley outside, the curtains billowed out and the darkness swayed.

'If this is a dream I like it,' he said. He felt more awake than in ages. Maybe this is how the longed-for comes true, sailing in at whatever time in the night, and you wake entirely calm and all you have to do is let it come ashore.

'Come on in, Stella,' he said.

She pulled back a curtain and let a pale light into the room. Perhaps it had been snowing while he slept. She peered down the alley towards the main street.

'Flags of convenience,' she muttered.

He waited and wondered how far gone she really was. She turned away from the window.

'You heard about the tanker?'

'Yes,' he said. 'Bad news waiting to happen.'

'I know the feeling,' she said and for a moment he thought she was maybe crying but it was not in character. 'Sorry,' she said, 'just wallowing.' She turned from the window and with only a slight list deposited herself on the edge of the bed.

He put his hand on her sleeve, felt a thin wet jacket and the lean hard arm underneath.

'Still raining out?' he asked.

'Hail and sleet,' she said. She was shivering. 'Blowing a hoolie, force ten maybe. The tanker won't last long in this and the tide's up right across the South Ness road. Folk are out with sandbags but their houses drain straight into the sea, so when the sea's higher than the drains, well . . .'

'So you can't get home?'

'It'll turn in a peedie while,' she said. 'It always does.'

He'd never heard her so subdued. When he'd met her at Johny Doo's party she'd never stopped wisecracking, fast tongue in a long mouth in a quick mind in a bendy body. She mocked the host's trousers, caricatured his taste in music, abused his joint-rolling abilities, danced with everybody and tripped as many as she could and ended up wrestling with Johny in the fireplace which was fortunately unlit. And when the evening turned mellow and the fiddles turned to Country & Western, she'd shouted, 'More pain, more pain! More loss, more dead dogs!' and collapsed still grinning on the hearthrug. The guys were queuing to help her home when the party broke up but somehow she'd slipped away with Ingrid and her sister and the last he saw of them was a swaying threesome clutching bottles liberated from the party, setting out towards the pier-head and she was waving her bottle at the moon and still calling out 'More pain, ya bass!'

'She was at school wi us afore she went Sooth,' Johnny

had said as they'd cleared up. 'We gave her a hard time when she wis peedie because her family wis strange and her being an incomer though her gran wis a Rendall frae Evie. Bloody hell, that's the last of the Highland Park she's aff wi. Ach, she's a great laugh, Stella. Naebody takes offence.'

Malcolm threw the last empties into the bin.

'So just what's she angry about?'

He didn't know why he'd said that, but he knew it was a bad sign because she was his sort of trouble. Maybe he'd take a wander down the pier just in case. With luck he wouldn't find *her*.

'It always does,' Stella said again. 'Then I'll be offski.'

A gleam of teeth like surf through the dark and he smelled gin and hash and cigarette smoke as she laughed quietly. The smell of late parties and indiscretion, it was not unpleasant on her.

'You smell like an illicit still,' he said.

'Illicit,' she repeated. 'I'm trying to put that behind me. Flags of convenience . . .'

'What's with these flags?'

'Everyone's flying one. Married man, single parent, party girl, problem child . . . To see what we can get off with. Or who . . .'

He wondered how out of it she was or if this was another mask. He'd seen her try on and discard enough of them in the last few weeks. He put his hand on her back. The other evening when she'd suggested they wrestle because he was shaking in her company, she hadn't thrown him but he'd found it a very strong back.

She straightened up.

'I've had a bit of a shock and I was coming past your door . . .' she said.

'You're soaking. Want to get in?'

'I'll go in a minute.'

She pulled off her jacket and trainers and got under the duvet. Her jeans were damp against his leg. He put his arm round her shoulders and her hand drifted across his chest, circled for a bit and met his hand. They lay on their backs and were silent.

'Look,' he said, 'I'm glad you're here but we can't . . . We mustn't.'

'I know,' she said. 'Anyway, it's not a good time for me.'

They lay for a while and she got warm and he was drifting between sleep and awake when the hands started to rise and slide of their own accord, like weed caught on a rising tide. The window shook as hail drilled against the glass. He could feel the big pane bulge in the dark, wondered how much it could take before it gave way and the night was into the room.

'This shock,' he said. 'Tell me about it.'

'Just another late session with too much alcohol and dope. It's hard to explain . . . These people I've known since school, mostly sons and daughters of the inner circle here, the fishermen and farmers and councillors and local businessmen. Solid people, you know? Mostly married, some with bairns, but still not quite ready to . . .'

She trailed off. When his hands stopped moving, hers did too. It was like she was following him down a street at night.

'Anyway, I was having this interesting talk with this guy, you wouldn't know him, about people and masks and the tanker, and I'm thinking this is good, this is where I want to be, with these solid real people, then I get up to go to the loo and he grabs my crotch. I was so shocked I just looked at him, I mean I thought we'd sorted all that – and then he does it again. And I get to the loo and there's a woman I know who's recently married and she's arranging to go off for a drive in the moonlight with the young guy from next door. I mean, come on! And when I get back to the party it seems like they're all at it and things are falling apart these days because we're all greedy bastards who pretend we're not in control so we can get our bit thrill. And I see Magnus slipping out the door with this wee lassie

I know is still at school, and his bairn that I babysit is upstairs asleep . . . Oh, it's disgusting!'

He nodded, picturing the party and the full tide outside and how when the sea gets higher than the drains all the waste and shit and everything you thought you'd got rid of flows back in.

'So you came here,' he said.

'I just wanted to get home and stop all this excess and get some purity and discipline into my life. Get some decent work done. But the tide was up and this guy was after me and I saw your door.'

Her hands were moving again. He lay and let it happen.

'Why are you afraid of me?' she asked.

'Should I be?'

'Your stomach's tense.'

'It's been a while,' he said. 'Should I be?'

'My boyfriend – my ex boyfriend – would say so. A disaster waiting to happen, he'd say. I get interested by people who seem strong and complete, and then I realize they're only pretending and then I lose interest and they start getting in touch with their feelings and learn to cry and then I want to be a million miles away.'

'Well I'm not your boyfriend and I'm not scared of you. Or complete,' he added quietly.

'Good,' she said. 'In that case . . .' She wriggled out of her jeans then sat up and pulled off her sweater. She did it cross-armed, gripping the bottom end then peeling it off over her head in one smooth gesture, shook her hair free and he knew he was in trouble. The hail punched the window and the glass creaked as she hesitated then pulled off her T-shirt.

'You're lovely,' he said. 'And I'm desperate to touch you. Only we can't.'

He saw the paleness turn his way, then a gleam of her eyes.

'Yes,' she said, but she was over him anyway and it was too late to protest and anyway he didn't want to and he still felt calm and solid like a long reef. She rose above him in the half light, a figurehead he thought, her face calm and dispassionate and concentrating into the distance till she finally lurched sideways and grounded herself, and though it was not a sensible time he could not stop flowing.

She stirred.

'God, I'm wrecked,' she said and slid away.

He heard her dressing and muttering to herself. Dawn was coming in but the gale sounded strong as ever.

'Shall I make tea?'

'No thanks,' she said and sat on the side of the bed and bent over him. He wanted to raise his hand and feel her breast and claim the experience again, or at least have her admit that it had happened. She put her hand on his chest and pushed herself upright.

'The tide will be down and I can go home now. Catch you later.'

'I'm going up to Shetland for a few days. Council business and seeing a friend.'

'Catch you later,' she said again and he heard her going down the stairs as he lay with the damp sheet and her strong back and calm administering face rocking over him.

He went quickly to the window and looked down the stone-flagged alley in time to see her hesitate at the corner of Victoria Street. A volley of hail swept down the street and she turned her head aside. He saw her hand come across her collar and pull up a hood.

The hood blew away. He saw – he felt – her resignation as she pushed off into the gale funnelling down the main street. She was leaning forward at such an angle that if the wind suddenly stopped, she'd fall on her face. And then she was gone and he was shivering.

He went back to bed and lay among the leakage and the shambles. He saw her face turning from the stinging hail and her voice saying 'It's disgusting!' but her hands saying the opposite, and he lay waiting for it to get as light as it ever would that winter.

'We don't like it being called a disaster here,' Ronnie said. 'It could have been, but it wasn't. Light crude and these gales – the oil's just disappeared. We want our compensation, but it's as important that we keep our reputation. We're so far from the markets here, man. Purity is all we've got going for us.'

'There's a tractor blocking the road.'

'Aye, we get out here and walk to the headland.'

They wrapped up and stumbled into the wind across the wet turf and over the ruts where the press and coastguard Land Rovers had come and gone. By the farmyard there'd been two fields of grey-topped turnips. Malcolm bent and pulled up some grass and rubbed it across his fingers. It looked alright. Maybe there was a slight greasiness. On the beaches they'd walked that morning he hadn't seen a single dead bird.

'Disappeared doesn't necessarily mean gone,' he said.

'For sure. We're testing all the time. It certainly hasn't got to my cages yet.'

'But in the long term?'

'Too early to say. Like HIV, right?'

Malcolm shivered and pulled his hat down over his ears. It was only a small gale but a cold one. He sniffed the air. Faint, but unmistakable.

'At first we smelled it as far as Brae, even up in Unst. But that was a good sign, meant it was evaporating. All that gas-mask nonsense – the press handed them out to kids then took the pictures.'

They came to the top of the rise and looked down. The rocks below looked familiar but something was missing.

'This is the right place?'

'I reckon so. As seen on TV.'

'But there's nothing here!'

'They say all the rivets popped. There's a lot of sheet metal lying on the sea bed. Ships that pass, eh?'

Mal shook his head as they hurried down to the rocks. The whole thing seemed so unlikely, like it had never happened.

He peered among the rocks looking for traces.

Here at the epicentre the rocks were darker and more slippy and that was about all. There was a fair swell running and maybe the waves were smoother than they should be. He saw what he was looking for, glinting in a greasy pool, bent down and put them in his pocket.

Ronnie shook his head and laughed. 'Bloody souvenir hunters,' he said.

'I want a reminder.'

'We don't forget, but now we get on with it.'

'Shetlanders! You raise stoicism to an art form.'

'So would you if you lived here. How's Orkney working out? You going to stay?'

Mal glanced at him, then out to sea. He wasn't sure about those waves. It was hard to remember what was normal.

'I like the job and the people,' he said. 'I'll wait and see.'

Ronnie nodded. 'There's work for you here if you want it. And even a few single women if you're interested.'

'Let's get back,' Mal said. 'It's bloody freezing.'

'Like that, is it?'

'Too early to say, pal.'

They walked back across the headland then cut across to Quendale Bay. He'd swum there with Ron and his kids two summers back. Very clear green water, very white sand. He'd felt free and happy and almost young.

The beach wasn't white now, but stained like the coal beaches of Fife. He dug into the sand. The stain went down a long way.

'You'll not be swimming with the bairns here for a while.'

'Na. But the kids had a great time sorting through the bruck for souvenirs.'

'Find anything interesting?'

Ronnie picked up a piece of thick board and handed it to him. 'Probably some plywood panelling from a cabin. You can keep it as a breadboard or cut it up and sell it to the touries from South.'

'Can't you take stoicism too far?'

Ronnie flipped the board onto the grass and looked at him. 'Fifteen hundred birds, a few fields, a handful of seals and four otters, one killed by a film crew's Land Rover. As for our fishing industry, it's too early to say. We'll damn well get our compensation and we'll demand changes till we get them, but we don't whinge and we'll not be media fodder.'

'Sorry I asked.'

Ronnie gripped his upper arm and smiled. 'Job's still there if you want it. Leaving South was the best thing me and Liz ever did.'

'So long as I don't have to grow a craw's nest on my face like yours.'

'The beard's not essential. Just don't talk about the Shetland Oil Disaster, right?'

They scrambled up from the beach. By the time they got to the car the light was fading and there was no smell any more.

He didn't knock because only strangers did. The rest put their head in the door and hollered. He went quickly up the stairs feeling entitled, chapped on her workroom door and went in.

She straightened up from her typewriter and pushed her headband back with both hands. She smiled slightly and her eyes were grey-blue and wide open, but he was at the door with his hands in his tweed coat and she at the desk, and the hands didn't seem ready to connect.

'Saw you coming up the street,' she said.

He nodded and slowly unbuttoned his coat. 'Thought you might. So what are you working at?'

'The usual. Earning my crust with *The Orcadian* and writing nippy stories about my friends.'

'Which is this?'

He hated when all he did was ask questions. She put a file over the typewriter.

'A nippy story.'

He went to look out the window. He'd never been in this room in the daytime, but the days were pretty short. From up here she could look right down the long twisting street, see everyone coming but they'd have to look up to spot her at this small high window. She did like control. His right arm was by her shoulder. Her hands were rolling a cigarette. What was the etiquette of this?

'Pull up a chair,' she said.

He did. He estimated the gap at thirty centimetres and closing. Same old jeans, same high arched eyebrows, same long crooked mouth that had descended on him.

'Well, hi,' she said. 'How was Shetland?'

'Not what I expected. I've been thinking of you.'

She nodded as though that was expected. She leant across twenty centimetres and kissed the side of his mouth. Then she sat back and lit up. He could see her calmly rolling above him in the near-darkness, he could see her grinning to herself as she withdrew the cigarette in broad daylight.

'You know how some things look worse from a distance?' She nodded. 'They've been let off, it's almost a miracle. In fact some of the local evangelicals are claiming the credit. Apparently God needed a Shetland prayer meeting to point out the situation to Him and He sent even bigger gales to clean up the mess.'

She laughed as he'd hoped.

'Take that coat off and tell me the rest,' she said.

She uncrossed her ankles and swung her long legs from the table.

'So it's a case of nearly but not quite,' she said. 'Could

have been but wasn't.' She looked at him then at the type-writer then out the window. He waited. 'By the way, I'm not pregnant.'

'Congratulations,' he said. 'It's been on my mind. That was absolutely bloody daft of us.'

'I'm terrified of having kids, but my body keeps trying to do this to me. There's bound to be an accident some day.'

He put his arm across her back. 'Only if you let it.'

She leaned forward and his arm slipped down. Long, warm, strong back.

'I was young, I was drunk, it was very dark,' she said.

'And the tide was high.'

'And the tide was excessively high. The usual excuses.'

So they looked at each other a while.

'I'd better get on with things,' she said.

'I've lots to do,' he said.

They stood up. She kissed him but her lips didn't part.

'When it's right,' she said, 'when it's really right and not a pleasant mistake, the only apparatus required is a sheet anchor.'

'Meaning?'

'Meaning there's no way of stopping, only of slowing down a bit. If it was right, we'd be on the bed already and we're not, so . . .'

'I never asked you to stumble into my room at five in the morning.'

'That was silly and I'm sorry. But we got off with it and now that's out of the way we can relax.' She put her hand on his arm as he reached for his coat. 'Now I don't have to perform for you and you don't have to perform for me. I could do with a good friend here, someone who doesn't lech after me or know me from school as some kind of arty weirdo.'

He buttoned up the coat, tightened the belt. When she said true things the damage dispersed, for a while.

'Too early to say if I can do that,' he said. 'I've been offered a job in Shetland when my contract's up with the harbour authority.'

She took the file off the typewriter. 'I'm a loyal friend,' she said. 'And I'm a lousy person to want. Or I'm a very bad enemy.' She glanced up at him. 'Your choice.'

He adjusted his scarf. 'That's a nice wee bit speech,' he said. 'You must have used it a few times.'

She shook her head and seemed delighted. 'You see?' she said. 'Some smart clerk to catch me out when I'm being phoney. That's all I'm asking. And I really can be good fun.'

'Oh aye,' he said. 'I've seen that.'

He opened the door. She was already having trouble keeping her eye off the page in the typewriter. A figurehead. An oddly beautiful figurehead with too much dark stuff behind. He reached in his pocket.

'Present for you from Shetland.'

'What for?'

'For the memory.'

He flipped the matchbox to her. It rattled in the air and she caught it one-handed. She shook it at her ear. She seemed delighted as a child.

'Not a bad memory,' she said.

He paused in the doorway as she opened the box and peered into it.

'Could have been worse,' he said and left.

At the end of the street he looked back up at her window. He could see her dimly through the glass, head propped on one hand, the other hand holding her hair back off her face. She was still looking down at the box.

The wind ran down his neck as he shrugged and turned up Hellihole Road, out of her sight if she was watching, which she wasn't. She was poking the little dull metal rivets round and round the box. She felt the resignation-feeling settling round her shoulders like a Shetland shawl, a familiar, secure feeling, and its pattern had a name: Nearly, but not quite.

She put the box aside, blew on her fingers and settled back to typing. If no one else came she'd finish it tonight.

At the top of the road he turned into the Braes Hotel, hoping for a game of pool with the Heriot Watt students or just a quiet pint with a view of nothing very much happening in the Sound of Hoy. He wondered if he'd be in her nippy story and whether he'd be relieved or miffed if he was not.

WALK ON

Jean Rafferty

Lily liked the library. It was just that lately she had begun to think it was too small for her. It was only a branch library in a dreary suburb anyway, but nowadays it seemed to be full of exhibitions by local schoolchildren, rack upon rack of videos, tables piled high with leaflets on Yoga for Beginners and a photocopier that Lily was always banging into. Of course that could have been because her hips were now forty-six inches.

The day that Miss Beaver herself drew attention to her size was the day that Lily decided she would quit. Not straight away of course. She knew she would have to find something else to do, which was not an easy task now that we were in the midst of recession.

Miss Beaver was the chief librarian and a lady of not inconsiderable proportions herself. She had glossy brown hair like her namesake and a shiny pink face that had never been subjected to makeup. Lily always wished Miss Beaver had little whiskers, but her face was smooth and hairless, though she did have a slightly evident over-bite. Not enough to call her Beaver-teeth out loud, but enough for Lily to be able to chant it to herself when Miss Beaver acted autocratically, which was not, admittedly, often.

When Miss Beaver did mortally offend her Lily would think of the darker implications of her name. How could anyone expect to be taken seriously with a name that signi-fied the female pudenda? There was a rankness, a wetness, a casual decadence about this connotation that always seemed completely at odds with Miss Beaver's scrubbed clean soul.

Lily knew that Miss Beaver must inevitably be the possessor of, well, a beaver, but delicacy prevented her from thinking about it, except when she was very angry. Then Miss Beaver's face would be transmogrified, slashed across with vaginal lips instead of her own moist, red mouth; a track of pubic hair sprouting across her round cheeks. Lily's anger never extended quite as far as visualizing Miss Beaver's beaver in its correct location.

Lily's best friend's brother was always cornering her and telling her about the Beaver Eaters' Club of which he was a member. Sarah, the best friend, and her mother Irene had no idea what he was talking about and always laughed as if it were a nonsensical piece of surreal humour. But Lily had read plenty of American novels in quiet moments at the library and would sometimes get very hot and red when she saw Richard approaching. So much so that Irene was convinced Lily had a secret crush on her son, something she found entirely understandable, though few outside his immediate family would have thought Richard a suitable object of passion. He was after all a teenage boy, of the boils and braggadocio variety.

Lily's best friend Sarah was as thin as Lily was fat. She, too, worked in a library, or an archive, as she called it. It kept records of shipping transactions and shipping lanes and other shipping arcana that Lily couldn't even begin to imagine. The two shared a flat with three other girls in the leafy suburb where Lily's library was situated. The flat was one of about twelve in a large Victorian house which used to be a family home. There was a pretty, communal garden at the back though there were many peculiarly shaped rooms where the developers had squeezed extra walls in. Lily had a trapezoidal bedroom.

Sarah had a wonderful bone structure. Lily envied her most of all for her jawline, which was clearly etched, without a tremor of surplus tissue. In middle years Sarah would

wear Jaeger and pearls and have a pack of dogs at her
heels. For now she wore a Burberry, her most treasured
possession, which she had got for £8 in a Sue Ryder shop.
To go with her upper-class appearance Sarah had adopted
a crystalline upper-class accent which was quite unlike the
way her mother and brother spoke, but so suited her looks
and style that it was they who seemed inauthentic and not
Sarah.

When Lily bewailed the glandular problem which had
led her to her current state of obesity, Sarah murmured
sympathetically and forbore to mention that Lily was capable of eating a double portion of pasta drenched in creamy
cheese sauce, accompanied by a sizeable chunk of golden
garlic bread, followed by a luscious slice of chocolate fudge
cake, heated slightly in the communal microwave and
topped with extra thick double cream from Marks and
Spencer's.

Sarah's lean body was always hunched in the cold,
against which she seemed to have no defence. Lily supposed
this was because she merely picked at food. Her appetites
lay in another direction. On Monday, Wednesday and Friday her boyfriend Simon, an accountant in a rather lack-
lustre firm, owned by a family of which he was not a
member, arrived to take her out, usually to the theatre or
the tennis club. He would then stay the night in the messy
bedroom which was so at odds with Sarah's elegant
outward appearance. There was not a spare inch of
surface space on the floor, which was always covered with
Sarah's clothes, dropped right where she stepped out of
them.

On Tuesday, Thursday and Saturday Sarah's other boyfriend, Tom, an engineer in a thrusting oil firm, arrived to
take her out, usually to the pub or the cheap-and-cheerful
curry restaurant just off the High Street. He, too, would
stay the night, though he was less sanguine about the mess.
Sarah would wave him away in protest. 'I haven't got time
for all that,' she would say, doubtless dreaming of some

time in the future when she could leave such matters to the domestic help. Lily thought the confusion in her bedroom might be symptomatic of confusion in her soul, but she wasn't sure as Sarah actively seemed to enjoy having two lovers.

Simon knew of Tom's existence though Tom was not sure of Simon's. Lily had decided this was because Simon was much sweeter natured than the rather taciturn Tom, who would doubtless explode with possessiveness if he knew about his rival. She sometimes suspected that Sarah thought of Simon as a wimp who could be treated in a more cavalier fashion than stubborn Tom.

The day Miss Beaver insulted her they were both stacking the shelves. Lily was bending over to move some Biggles books from the lower shelves when she backed into Miss Beaver. Miss Beaver sighed. 'You know, Lily, bumping into you these days is like being battered with pink blancmange.'

Lily was mortified. She shoved the books into Miss Beaver's hands. 'And another thing,' she yelled. 'We shouldn't have these in the library. They're racist.'

That night she bought herself a big bag of Kettle Chips and a bottle of red wine. She sat in the garden in the dark. It was high summer and still warm, though she draped a voluminous shawl her mother had crocheted for her round her shoulders. Mary and Fanny in number two were having a dinner party and she could hear the laughter of their guests, the clink of their glasses. She poured a huge shot of Chilean Cabernet into her own wineglass and raised it in their direction. Two rooms along from them came the sound of moaning. Sarah's bedroom and Saturday, so it was Tom tonight. Although Sarah was languid in her everyday life she was a furnace of energy in the bedroom. Her abandoned cries made Lily feel dull, a failure. She bit savagely into a Kettle Chip.

It seemed to her out there in the garden, on her own, that life could be a very lonely business at times. All around her were the sounds of enjoyment, even of ecstasy. Clinking cutlery, bottles opening with a pop, people joking and laughing and nibbling and nuzzling. And the cacophony of sounds that signified human love, the grunts and gasps and groans that made the whole process seem so brutal, so ugly, when you were not the one . . .

At number two the evening had progressed to music. 'Just listen to this,' said a man's voice, thick with drink and drunk with emotion. 'You won't believe it's that bloody football song.' In the dark Lily could smell the white roses. Their scent was sharp but heavy, but with that deep deep potency that seems, in roses, to be dredged up from the very heart of the earth. 'When you walk through the storm, Hold your head up high, And don't be afraid of the dark.'

Here she was in the dark and Lily was no longer afraid. The voice coming from the flat was fine spun, delicate, as if the sound came floating effortlessly off the surface of the tongue. It was a voice produced as birds produce sound, simply by opening their throats. It was so beautiful Lily could hardly bear it, but there was something unthinking about it too. It was not the voice of a person who had suffered.

Lily scrambled up, knowing that if she were to sing, the sound would have to come from somewhere else in her body. She planted her feet solidly on the ground, crunching the rest of the Kettle Chips in her haste. The choir were singing now, an octave lower than the soprano. 'At the end of the storm there's a golden sky, and the sweet silver song of the lark.' Lily could feel her shoulders dropping, her spine elongating. 'Walk on, walk on,' she urged, her voice soaring up there with the singer, surprising her. 'With hope in your heart. And you'll never walk alone.' The words were banal, yet to Lily they said what she felt. She was walking through the storm and she wouldn't give up and one day she would come to the end of it. Hope, hope. She seemed to have no trouble reaching the high notes. In fact she liked singing them so much she could hardly let them go. She sang another chorus after Kiri Te Kanawa had finished.

A window flew up and several people peered out of number two but they couldn't see her in the dark of the garden. They shrugged and went in again. 'Probably a cat.'

'That was brilliant,' said a voice in her ear. Just her luck, thought Lily. A Saturday-night drunk.

'This is a private garden, you know,' she said.

'I do know, my nightingale,' he replied. ''Cos I live here. Aren't you offering your new neighbour a little drinkie-poo?' He held up the remains of her Chilean red.

'Help yourself,' said Lily. She didn't care any more about the drink anyway.

'You should go on the stage,' said the new neighbour.

Maybe I will, thought Lily. Why not?

Her first stop was the amateur theatrical section at the library. There were several books on voice production which she took home with her. But she felt silly trying out the exercises in her room. Hah, hah, hah, hah. Hee, hee, hee, hee.

'Lily. Are you all right in there?' called Sarah sharply.

Next morning she frowned as she crunched her muesli with dainty teeth. 'That was a right caterwauling last night,' she said severely. 'Simon found it rather unromantic, as a matter of fact.'

'Tough,' said Lily. Up till now she had favoured Simon's suit, but she reckoned nothing would put Tom off once he was in the throes of passion and thought there was something to be said for that.

'Well, that's rather a selfish attitude, I must say,' said Sarah.

'What would you know? You're just a Hitchcock blonde who's too dim to know her own mind.'

They didn't speak for three days after that, until Lily relented and apologized. She thought Sarah was looking a bit peaky and decided she would have to be kinder to her. By that time she had found herself a voice coach and could afford to be magnanimous. The coach's name was Violet and she worked out of her own little flat near the railway line. She always wore jogging suits, though she was a woman well ensconced in middle age. She said they freed the voice. She had been a singer herself, playing minor roles in a famous opera company. She was always the servant, the companion.

'Didn't you get fed up, always watching someone else get the applause?' asked Lily, as countless others had before her.

'I was good enough to *be* there,' said Violet. 'Not many people are.'

She listened to Lily, head cocked to one side like a curious bird. 'Not bad,' she said, nodding her startling crest of blonde corkscrew curls as Lily did her first set of scales. 'But you're a big girl. Stop standing as if you're a small one.'

Obediently, Lily tried to stand up straight, as her mother had always told her to, but Violet unexpectedly laughed. 'I didn't mean that,' she said. 'I meant you're *big*. Solid. Anchor your weight to the floor. Let me see you use it.' Lily blushed, but Violet was oblivious to it. 'I'm just a little thing. You should be able to make me scared of you.'

Lily thought it extremely unlikely that anyone would ever be scared of her. Even when she loomed above the other children at school she had been the butt of the jokes. 'Fatso, fatso, crazy, crazy,' they all sang at her, to the tune of some Italian song whose words they'd hijacked. Her father was always very concerned on her behalf but her mother usually told her to straighten her backbone and fight.

They lived in a quiet town in the Home Counties, where Lily's father was the local vicar. He was a somewhat vague man who was nevertheless capable of physical feats requiring great willpower and endurance. His skin had the glow of a man who regularly hiked for miles in Derbyshire's Peak District. Lily and her mother restricted themselves to pottering gently round famous gardens.

Lily's mother was somehow more problematical. She was a small, wiry woman, who ate sparingly and made Lily feel like some monstrous cuckoo crowding out a sparrow's nest. She was moderate in everything, a trait Lily found hard to bear. For years she suffered agonies of embarrassment at being the dowdiest girl in the school, simply because her mother had a passion for thrift. Before Green politics were ever invented she was recycling clothes – turning collars; putting false hems on skirts that were already, in Lily's eyes, too long; replacing linings. 'There,' she'd say proudly, ignoring or ignorant of the fact that the results of her efforts were usually ghastly. 'That's perfectly serviceable now.'

Ever since, Lily had craved more than the merely service-able. She longed for the gorgeousness of silk, the softness of cashmere, for swirly prints and tropical colour and dangling earrings and drama. At work she settled for a neat, navy blue suit. But she knew there was something more. Not merely material things which you could label and say, I want this. Just something more.

Her father would have put a label on it and said she was looking for God, but Lily wasn't interested. God was too long-standing a concept for her to feel she had much invested in it, or Him. She suspected He might have lost His usefulness nowadays. Nor was she interested in love, at least not as an absolute, not as a solution to the 'problem' of a woman's life. Nor in money. Nor in children. Lily knew that one or other of these things preoccupied most of the rest of humanity and that she was, therefore, odd. But what could she do about it? That was the way she was.

Violet made her feel that the something more might be reachable. It was not that she praised her voice or told her she would have a glittering career. But Lily worked, at first a couple of nights a week and then eventually every night after the library. And, as she worked, she felt a sense of wonder at the voice that was emerging from deep inside her. She, who had stumbled and stuttered her way through library life, now found a power she hadn't known she possessed.

In the library she found herself decisive where once she had been tentative. Now she was the one who would tackle the rowdy schoolboys.

'Fuck off, fatso,' they said to her one Monday afternoon, but she didn't falter. She simply stood beside them and let her weight flow into the ground, as Violet had taught her. Then she drew the breath up from her stomach. In a menacing tone she said, 'Out.' Much to her own and Miss Beaver's surprise, they went. 'Well done, my dear,' she said, but it was too late for Lily to care.

At home she began to dress herself in the type of clothes she had always wanted to wear. She got them mostly from the thrift shop, her Paisley-patterned shawls and flowing dresses. She moved to the tinkling sound of the glass bracelets she got from an Indian bazaar in Balham High Road. Finally, she dyed her hair a magnificent auburn. Her mother would have been hard put to recognize her, but Lily felt more distinctly herself than she had ever been.

Often, as she left for her voice class in the evening (where Violet made her remove the jangling bangles) her drunken neighbour from the garden would join her. He was no longer drunk, of course. In fact Lily found it difficult to see the ebullient inebriate of that night in the rather solemn young man who walked along beside her, seemingly fascinated by everything she said or did. His name was William, never Will, which was too racy for him, or Bill (too blokeish). Behind the horn-rimmed glasses his sharp bright eyes took in every detail of Lily's not-yet-complete transformation.

Soon, he took to collecting Lily from her class and they

would call in at the pub on the way home. They only had one drink, which they would pay for turn and turn about. William would straighten his already ramrod back as they went in and lift his chin with pride that he was accompanied by such a grand example of womanhood.

One night the landlord nodded in Lily's direction as William waited at the bar. 'I bet she's a prime piece of rump,' he said lasciviously.

'I beg your pardon,' said William in his snootiest voice, but later he invited Lily into his flat for coffee and later still they ended up in bed together.

This was something of a revelation to Lily. She had a suspicion that, with his weedy-looking frame and swot's glasses, William was considered one of life's nerds, but she found herself entranced by his body, the ribs etched against his skin as he turned away from her, the discrete muscles visible in his shoulder. He, for the first time in her life, made her feel that her body was beautiful. 'You're so soft,' he sighed, rolling his face in her stomach like a cat rolling in grass. She was young and her skin was still springy to the touch, as it would not be were she this fat later on in life. For now, worshipped by William, she ceased to think of herself as ugly. She rubbed her now forty-two-inch hips against the polyester sheet, offered up the creamy sponginess of her breasts to her lover. She felt that she was ample.

Her metamorphosis into a socially acceptable human being was completed with an invitation to a dinner party at number two. Sarah raised an eyebrow in surprise when Lily told her. 'Well, at least you'll enjoy the food,' she said. 'Mary's a cordon bleu cook.' Lily did. Often in the past she had played the fat person's gambit of non-existent appetite, the pretence 'I really couldn't,' when it's plain to see you really could – and could manage half a hog, three pounds of mashed potatoes and a box of chocolates besides.

Tonight, she savoured every dish that was put in front

of her, eating no more than anyone else but no less either. She felt sophisticated. The marinated fish, the Moroccan lamb with quinces, the spun sugar confection with raspberries all seemed to her to be elegant and exceptional, as she felt the people round the table were. And when they asked her to sing Lily knew that she was going to hit all the notes perfectly. Some spirit of devilment made her choose 'You'll Never Walk Alone' for this, her debut in front of an audience. Not only because she knew it was within her range, but because it amused her to think that these same people had unwittingly compared her to a cat.

As she stood to sing it occurred to her there was an element of nosiness in their asking her to perform. Everybody in the flats knew that she was spending all her cash on voice lessons. How ridiculous she would look if she could not sing properly. Lily, for all the camaraderie of the evening, suddenly felt sad. But perhaps it was better that way. This song she had chosen was not, for all its message of hope, a happy song. There was in it some sense of defiance, of determination in the face of despair, which was why aggressive football supporters had appropriated it.

Lily must not only wipe out all thoughts of these louts. She must find a way to make the defiance pure, the hope spiritual. She made herself go very still. The others were there and not there. She wanted to sing *for* them, but they didn't matter. What mattered was the power inside, that she must honour. She knew that if she did that, she would be giving a gift to them.

Standing there in the middle of the cramped room, candles guttering in the wine bottles, she sensed she made a ridiculous figure, a fat girl with lurid dress sense. But she didn't care. From the depths of her stomach she dredged the sounds, let the notes resonate round her diaphragm before releasing them joyously into the stuffy atmosphere. Hold your head up high. She felt like the statue she had seen on a school trip to Paris. The Winged Victory of

Samothrace, looming massive at the head of the Louvre stairs. It didn't matter that her head was missing. Her face was Lily's face, the face of all the women who looked on her and wanted to rush headlong, like her, towards triumph. Walk on, walk on, with hope in your heart. Lily felt her voice lifting her like wings.

When she finished there was a sense of unease in the room. They were unnerved by their own feeling of awe. It was with relief that someone suddenly remembered to clap. Mary, the cordon bleu cook, had tears in her eyes. 'I've never heard anything like that,' she said. William smiled proudly over at her. She could tell he was aching to go to bed with her. She laughed to herself. Really, she would have liked to sing all night.

Later, when they left, William put his hand somewhere near her waist. As soon as their hosts' door closed he pulled her in to face him. They were kissing like teenagers when over William's shoulder Lily saw Sarah stumbling up the stairs, tears streaming down her face. Alarmed, she pushed William away. 'Lily!' he protested. As she followed Sarah into the flat she noted with amusement that his glasses had literally steamed up.

Sarah had flung herself into a kitchen chair and was sobbing, head down on the crumby table. 'Sarah. Sarah. What on earth's the matter?'

Sarah wrung her nose with her forefingers. 'Got any paper hankies?'

Lily, as always in times of trauma, reached for the kettle. 'Oh, go to bed, William,' she said crossly as her lover pounded on the door.

Sarah was distraught. 'Tom's found out about Simon,' she wailed. Tom had inadvertently phoned Sarah's office seconds after Simon, and Sarah had got confused. 'Now he says I've got to marry him or that's the end of it,' she said. 'And Simon says I've to marry *him*.'

'Most women would be delighted to have one proposal of marriage, never mind two,' said Lily.

'But now I really *will* have to make up my mind,' said Sarah.

'A list,' said Lily. 'That's what you do in these situations. You put down all the pros and all the cons.'

'All right,' said Sarah. 'Who first?'

'Simon,' said Lily firmly. She didn't want any time wasted on protocol. 'I think Simon's better looking than Tom.'

Sarah frowned. 'Yes, I suppose he is. Tom's craggier, though.'

'Craggy's a virtue now?' demanded Lily.

Sarah blushed. 'No, I suppose not.'

'Simon's got a steady job.'

'But Tom has much more money. He's got oodles of the stuff.'

'Has he?' Lily was surprised. She hadn't noticed Tom being particularly free with his cash.

'We could have a big house somewhere nice in Surrey, or Kent.'

'Simon's much sweeter natured, don't you think?'

'Yes, I suppose so. You don't find him just a touch bland?'

'He's always beautifully turned out.'

'I mistrust a man who spends too much time on his appearance.'

Lily had a strong desire to tell Sarah that Tom was an ill-mannered, grumpy boor who always fell asleep in his armchair. Instead she simply said, 'I don't think you need any help in making up your mind. I'd say you know who you want already.'

'Do I?' Sarah's habitually vague look was replaced by one of astonishment.

'Do you think we'll ever see each other when you're married and living in a big house in Surrey?'

'Of course we will,' said Sarah. 'Anyway, it won't be straight away.' She looked round the scruffy kitchen, at the scuffed lino on the floor, the scratched table where several generations of tenants had cut vegetables straight on to the surface without a chopping board. 'What do you think you'll do next?'

Lily was embarrassed. 'Well . . .'

'Perhaps you'll become a famous singer and be much too grand ever to come down and see us.

Lily tried a casual laugh but it came out as a sort of a croak.

'You'll probably marry William and come and live next door to us in Surrey,' said Sarah brightly.

William worked himself into a frenzy of passion over the next few months. He had a child's dislike of being shut out of anything. Lily began to miss her late-night chats with Sarah over a mug of coffee, but William was so sweet she wanted to make him happy. He was the cleverest man she had ever met. His pedantic, almost fussy manner hid a brilliant brain which could absorb endless amounts of information. You could read a page from the encyclopaedia and William would repeat it word for word. (This was one of his party tricks.) He knew the name of every bird in Britain and Europe, how computers worked, all the different permutations of chess opening theory. He had won a scholarship to Cambridge but his father had died and he had had to work to support his mother. Lily knew this was morally right but she thought it a great waste of William's intellect. He worked in a bank.

There came a day when Violet, Lily's singing coach, finally told her what she had been longing to hear. 'If you keep on working hard you'll really do it. You'll get much further than I ever did,' said Violet.

'As a professional, you mean?' asked Lily.

'Of course, you clot. We both know that's what we're aiming for.' Yes. It was a relief to have it out in the open.

That night, Lily was disappointed that William didn't come to meet her after class. It was the first time in a long time. She was dying to tell him her news and rushed home, but when she got there there was only Sarah, looking nervous. Lily knew something awful had happened. 'I'm really sorry,' said Sarah. 'I'm afraid your father's died.' It was so unexpected that Lily's face creased in a bizarre rictus of a smile. No. No. 'Your mother phoned. She sounds really strange. I'm so sorry, Lily.' Sarah took Lily's plump hand in her own cool one.

When Lily got to her parents' house it was filled with people from the parish. Her mother was ensconced in state in her father's leather armchair, which she had always hated. 'I told him he should get help with that garden,' she said, though in fact she had never said anything of the kind.

Through the endless tedium of the rituals, the cups of tea, the funeral preparations, the sympathetic phone calls, Lily began to sense that more than her father had died. In one sense the practical requirements of death were a relief. They took her mind off her father and how much she knew she would miss him. But the effort they required frightened her. She knew they were distracting her from dealing with the problem of her mother.

It was in the middle of the funeral that Lily knew for certain her mother *was* a problem. The pallbearers had just lurched through the church entrance, faces straining with the effort of carrying her father plus £1,200 of mahogany coffin. Lily felt sick. That dead weight seemed so final.

As the congregation sat down she wondered if she would faint. It was the first time any of them had stopped for breath in the last few days and she wasn't ready for the emotions that assailed her. The most extraordinary feeling of heat and nausea slid across her. She knew her cheeks were all red and puffy. Then her mother leaned across her auntie Bet and tapped her. 'Lily,' she said loudly. 'What are all these people doing in my house? Did you bring them here?'

When it was all over, auntie Bet told Lily that she *would* have taken her mother but her own gout was too bad now and she wouldn't be able to cope. There wasn't much money, of course, enough to get them limited nursing help and a small house in a rather dreary village. It took months to organize buying it and getting Lily a job in a local super-market. The village was just near enough for Lily to come up to town for the occasional concert, but too far away for her to be able to afford the fare to her suburban library. She felt quite sorry to go in the end. Miss Beaver said she'd always been a good worker, though over a second glass of Asti Spumante confessed she hadn't much liked Lily's bangles the last few months.

William had a look of relief on his face when she told him she was going. It turned out he'd met a middle-aged lady with epilepsy and a teenage son and was going to move in with them. Lily wondered what his position would be in the household. She rather thought William had turned out to be an eccentric, collecting peculiar lovers as other people collect butterflies or train numbers.

Violet was furious of course. 'What a waste,' she yelled. 'You're throwing your life away.' Lily thought bleakly of the mother she didn't even like. She knew she could never be so heartless as to put her in a home, especially because the thought was so tempting.

When Sarah married Tom a year later Lily agreed to sing at the wedding. Sarah particularly wanted the one Kiri Te Kanawa sang at Princess Diana's wedding, Handel's 'Let the Bright Seraphim'. 'It's so English,' she said.

Lily was satisfied. She felt she had come full circle. One of the circles of hell. Now, for a weekend at least, she would have freedom. Her mother had gone into respite care at a local hospital. No guilt this weekend at her own anger, no demands from an old lady in whom she hardly recognized her mother any more.

The organist played very precisely at the rehearsal, which pleased her. The song needed elegance. It was so full of difficult phrases. You had to have absolutely clear articula-tion and even then people would probably not know what

it was all about, because the words didn't mean much anyway. It was the music that made it so bright and hopeful.

Sarah was a beautiful bride. She had chosen ivory
coloured satin, cut in a severe line that suited her lean body.
Lily felt squashed into her own dress, a cerise silk creation
she had bought in happier times. Just before breakfast on
the morning of the wedding Lily had one of her asthma
attacks, but once the time came to sing she was all right.
For the first time in many months she felt happy.

'Let the bright Seraphim in bu-u-u-urning row, Their
loud uplifted angel trumpets blow.' Lily was glad she had
continued to do her voice exercises. Sometimes she felt a
bit silly standing in the middle of the dining room shouting
her head off, particularly when her mother came in and
glared at her for interrupting *Coronation Street*, but you
needed huge lung capacity to produce the dainty trills and
runs of this song. She attacked them with all the verve and
clarity at her disposal.

The middle section was easier vocally. 'Let the cherubic
host in tuneful choirs, Touch their immortal harps with
golden wires.' But standing there in the middle of the little
country church that Sarah had chosen for its picturesque
quality, though it was not her local parish, Lily had to fight
hard to control the choking feeling in the back of her throat.
Sun saturated the stone of the church and filled her with
heat. The passage was slow and beautiful, with that tinge
of sadness that the most moving music has. Lily found the
idea of a cherubic host absurd, yet she allowed herself to
be suffused with the idea of immortality. As her rich voice
slid into the minds of the congregation she felt herself to
be more than she was and yet less, an atom blowing in
an infinite wilderness. She was queerly comforted by the
thought.

Afterwards, she knew that people were talking about her.
She slipped her coat over the cerise silk so that no-one
would notice her.

'That girl could have been in the opera,' said Sarah's

mother, Irene, with a glow of pride that her daughter had such talented friends.

'It's such a pity she had to give up her training. She must be very fond of her mother,' said Mary, the gourmet cook from number two.

'God, didn't Lily look fat?' said Tom to his bride.

BIOGRAPHICAL NOTES

ALISON ARMSTRONG was born in Bradford, Yorkshire and now lives in Alloa. She is the winner of the 1994 *Cosmopolitan*/Basildon Bond Short Story Award. 'An Apt Conceit' marks her second appearance in *Scottish Short Stories*.

IAIN BAIN was born and brought up in Glasgow. He worked as an editor for ten years in Glasgow, Eastbourne and London. In 1989, he became a father, turned freelance and returned to his native city. He is probably still there, working on his novel, writing for, and playing in his band, looking after his son and, occasionally, working.

LYNNE BRYAN was born in England in 1961. She moved to Glasgow five years ago, after completing an MA in Creative Writing at the University of East Anglia. She currently works for a women's support project and was a founding director of the Scottish feminist magazine *Harpies & Quines*. Her work has appeared in a number of anthologies and magazines. She is currently writing a collection of short stories and a novella.

FELICITY CARVER was born in 1945, and lives in Edinburgh. The mother of two grown-up children, she is a painter and a writer, 'Sand' being her third story to appear in this collection. She has also published short stories in *Encounter* and *London Magazine*.

ANDREW COWAN was born in Corby in 1960. 'Terminus' is his second story to be published in this collection. *Pig*, his first novel, was winner of a Betty Trask Award in 1993, and a Ruth Hadden Award this year, and is published by Michael Joseph in August 1994. He lives in Glasgow with the writer Lynne Bryan and their daughter, Rose.

ANGUS DUNN was born in Clydebank in 1953, and raised in Aultbea and Cromarty. He attended Aberdeen University and subsidized his travelling with a variety of part-time jobs. Now living in Ross-shire, his short fiction has been published in *West Coast Magazine*, *Cencrastus* and *Northwords*.

G. W. FRASER was born in Burghead, Moray, in 1955. He now lectures in Physics at the University of Leicester. 'The Strange Marriage of

Albert Einstein and Philipp Lenard' is his second story to appear in this collection.

ANDREW GREIG was born in Bannockburn in 1951, was raised in East Fife, and now lives mostly in the Lothians and Orkney. He has published six books of poetry including *The Order of the Day* and *Western Swing* (Bloodaxe Books); two books on mountaineering in the Himalayas, and a novel, *Electric Brae* (Canongate).

ALEXANDER MCCALL SMITH is the author of some thirty books for children. His short stories have appeared in four previous editions of *Scottish Short Stories*. He is a Reader in Law at the University of Edinburgh.

LINDA MCCANN has published poetry and short stories and has been Writer in Residence for the Universities of Glasgow and Strathclyde. She lives in Glasgow.

DUNCAN MCLEAN was born in Aberdeenshire and now lives in Orkney. His first collection of stories, *Bucket of Tongues*, won a Somerset Maugham Award in 1993, and his first novel, *Blackden* will be published in September 1994 by Secker & Warburg.

CANDIA MCWILLIAM was born in Edinburgh in 1955. She is the author of *A Case of Knives* (1988), *A Little Stranger* (1989), and *Debatable Land* (1994).

GILLIAN NELSON was educated in Edinburgh and has lived near Inverness since 1980. She has worked as a teacher, is now a gardener and is married to a mathematician. She is currently working on *Northern Harbours*, a companion to her history of northern Scottish bridges, *Highland Bridges*. Her fifth novel, *Walking in the Garden*, was published in April this year.

FIONA PATTISON would like to thank her friend, Charlotte Davies, for finding the Potato that Never Was.

SYLVIA PEARSON was born in 1933 and lives in Edinburgh. She began her writing career in her mid-fifties and is currently working on a novel and a collection of South African short stories. 'The Garden-Boy' is her second story to appear in this collection.

JEAN RAFFERTY was brought up in Glasgow and has been a journalist for fifteen years. She is the author of two books on sport and is currently working on a short story collection.

ALI SMITH was born in Inverness, has lived in Aberdeen and Edinburgh and now lives in Cambridge, where she writes and teaches and tears tickets at a cinema. She has published drama, short fiction, poetry, criticism and reviews in a number of books and magazines. A collection of her short fiction will be published by Virago next year.

RUTH THOMAS was born in Kent in 1967 and has lived in Edinburgh since 1985. She has been writing short stories and poetry for a number of years, while working in a variety of part-time jobs, and was awarded a bursary by the Scottish Arts Council in 1992. She has also contributed stories to *New Writing Scotland, 1993* and *Rebel Inc.*

ALAN WARNER was born in Argyll in 1964 and works on the railways. 'A Dog's Life' is one of his earliest short stories. His novel, *Morvern Callar* will be published by Jonathan Cape in February 1995.

ESTHER WOOLFSON was born in Glasgow and educated at the Hebrew University of Jerusalem and Edinburgh University. She now lives in Aberdeen. 'At the Turn' is her fifth story to be published in this collection.